Love's Prey

Francesca Quarto

Love's Prey

Love's Prey by Francesco Quarto
© 2018 Love's Prey
Swartz Creek, MI 48473

Printed in the United States of America

Chapter 1

Tricia never intended to stay on the Reservation. She saw its drab and hopeless life suck the joy out of her mother and the other women in their close-knit family. They expected little more than husbands and children and lived a life of servitude to both.

Encouraged by Lionel Reed, Pastor of Outreach Ministries, she'd been working since graduation, the year before, toward a special endowment scholarship awarded to Native American women pursuing higher education. It would be her ticket out of the dead-end life she believed awaited her, otherwise.

The pastor's wife, Audrey Reed, enthusiastically supported his suggestion, thinking her husband's interest in bettering the young girl's life was a true expression of his unique mission. She arranged her schedule so she could pick Tricia up and give her a lift home, on Tuesdays and Thursdays, after normal closing hours. This would allow Tricia to continue her painting and drawings in the facility's art room, while Audrey worked on Center business.

One such evening, Tricia was surprised to see the tall, thin pastor at her door. He explained to her parents that his wife was ill and he'd be driving Trish back and forth.

She slipped into his SUV for the short ride to the Community Center. At first she thought he was staring at her chest, but then remembered he was a preacher and felt guilty for thinking such a thing. It was dark in the vehicle as soon as she shut the door and the dome light went out, so she must have been mistaken.

"I appreciate your taking me this evening, Reverend Reed," she said quietly as he drove toward the low, brick building silhouetted against the moonlit sky.

***

Reverend Reed parked in the Community Center's lot and hopped out to help Tricia carry her art books and supplies. They walked to the front door and he juggled her easel and a stack of books, and then handed her the keys so she could unlock the building. She passed close to him as she entered, and he inhaled the flowery scent of her freshly shampooed hair. The hallway light brought her slim form into sharp focus. She was wearing a thin, cream-colored blouse with a round neck, closed with a drawstring. Her jeans were tight, emphasizing a seductive swing of hips as she moved forward into the building, switching on lights as she went.

"I'll just go set my stuff up, Reverend Reed, and get started if you don't mind."

Without waiting for his reply, she moved toward the empty art room at the back of the building, waiting for him to follow with her materials.

He felt his hands getting moist as they clutched her art books and bulky easel. He could feel his heartrate rise with excitement.

He never believed he'd have the opportunity to be alone with this ravishing beauty. Her face and figure haunted his dreams on endless nights, bringing him to the verge of nervous exhaustion, afraid he might actually call out her name in his sleep. How would he explain such a thing to his wife? His wife. Her flu had been a convenient excuse for him to help out with some of her errands, such as this one, driving Tricia to work on her art. The young girl had become an obsession to him, and like all unattainable things one desires, the chance of disaster was all too real. He knew he had to act now and feed his mad craving, or he'd never be free of her hold over him.

Tricia was getting a fresh sketch pad from the bottom of a long cabinet. She looked up as he entered, oblivious to his churning emotional state.

"Usually, when your wife is here, we both work for two hours. So if you'd like to take off, I'll lock the door behind you and see you at ten."

"Actually, Tricia. I wanted to watch you work for a while," he said, looking around the room. "I-I've wanted to tell you…that is…show you…how important the art program is to me."

Tricia watched the face of the pastor color, and wondered if he was embarrassed. She stammered out the first thing that came to her mouth. "What do you mean? I don't understand."

They were in a small room, crowded with easels and a few desks and tables for supplies. She had nowhere to go, but when she bumped into a table she realized she'd been unconsciously backing away from the man's flushed face and fierce gaze that was now definitely fixated on her bosom. His hands kept opening and closing as if they were squeezing rubber stress balls.

"I need to show you how I feel. I have to let it out, or it will consume me as it has day after day since I first saw you!"

He sounded desperate and afraid. But there was something else, something sinister in the way his hands were moving.

She shifted her direction, but now the backs of her legs bumped against a low desk. Tricia looked down in desperation and saw a pair of long scissors, instinctively slipping them into her hand. She held the newfound weapon behind her back.

"You-you're scaring me. You need to stay away from me, Reverend Reed. Whatever you are feeling toward me, isn't right. It's not something I ever wanted." He took a step forward and she tried to reason with him, to make him realize what he was doing by saying, "Please, your wife is a good person and you don't want to hurt her."

His face contorted in anger and was covered in a sheen of perspiration. The bright overhead fluorescents highlighted dark smudges under his eyes, making him look more like a demon than a man of God.

He edged closer.

"It isn't her I need to hurt, it's you! I need to end your control over me, you little whore. Sashaying around here with your tight jeans and perky tits. Don't pretend you didn't know the effect you were having on me. Enough! You can't control my every waking moment any longer. But that means I must have you body and soul. Now! I'm going to pound your tender flesh until I get your out of my dreams or die trying."

Tricia's mouth fell open in shock. He lunged before she could react. Grabbing a fistful of her blouse, he wrenched it downward to her waist. She felt the rough jerk on her neck as the gauzy material gave way, leaving only the red drawstring, still tied in a bow around her throat. The sight of her full breasts spilling over the top of last year's pink lacey bra, the one her mom bought her for school at a big box store, along with the jeans that clung too tight to her now fully-developed female curves, seemed to stop him for a second. It was all the time Tricia needed to plunge the scissors into the Reverend's neck. They made a soft sucking sound as she tugged them free.

He looked shocked as his hand closed over the gaping wound. When he moved it to stare at the red wetness on his fingers, blood sprayed from his artery in a wide arc, splattering the wall and tables before covering the floor where he fell.

Tricia stood frozen by the scene as her would-be attacker bled out. She tried to think, but terror overwhelmed her. She stared wide-eyed at the carnage. The blood soaked Lionel Reed's clothes, though the pool around him had finally stopped growing. Watching his chest for even the faintest rise, she could find none.

Forcing herself to move, she circled around the dark pool, careful not to step into it. She glanced down to see that the scissors were still dripping with his blood. *I need to get away from here. No one would ever believe me if I tell them I was defending myself,* she thought franticly.

She dropped the scissors and began to gather up her art supplies and jam them into her box. *I can't run carrying this stuff,* she realized. She put it all back on the table where he placed them before the nightmare began.

Tricia turned to leave, but then bent to take only one thing from that room of death, the scissors. These she carefully wiped off with the sandy dirt behind the building. After putting them into her satchel-like purse, she began a long run toward the town, five miles away from the Res.

There was a Greyhound Bus Station there and Tricia needed to get as far away from the Res as she could. She had twenty-six dollars and loose change in her wallet. Enough for a ticket somewhere, anywhere.

She didn't think once about leaving her family and everything she ever knew behind. She just ran full-out through the gathering dusk. Her instincts were screaming for her to get away from the bloody scene and the fallen preacher.

Chapter 2

The moon sailed full and bright overhead. The wind picked up and whipped her long curls around her face as she ran blindly down the road. She passed out of the Reservation and onto the County road.

The only witness to her flight trailed her from the Center after smelling the rich blood splashed across the floor and seeped throughout the wood. Silhouetted against the backdrop of hills, he tracked the girl with the long raven hair, loping off to her left. He would intercept her as she rounded the next curve in the road. His lips pulled back over long fangs as he anticipated the sweetness of her moist flesh.

Tricia's heart thudded against her ribs, but she never slowed, despite her fear. Or perhaps because of it. Her dreams of using her artistic talent to escape the life of poverty and all its limitations on the Res had morphed into a nightmare where she ran for her life, not after a now-impossible dream.

She got a stitch in her side, stabbing at her breath like the scissors hidden in the bottom of her bag stabbed at her conscience. Thinking of them reminded her of the grisly scene she had left for others to discover. It would likely be the Center's secretary, Joan Little Feather, a wonderful, warm person, who found the mangled body. Tricia felt the sting of remorse at the thought of the sweet woman's horror at finding Reed's body lying in the dark puddle, but there was nothing to be done for it.

She ran on.

Up ahead, the road would take a sharp bend and then there would be no way anyone from the Res could possibly see the running figure.

Tricia took deep, ragged breaths as she reached the curve. She slowed her pace to a jog. She'd always been a strong runner in school and had a reputation for remarkable endurance, but she wanted to conserve enough energy to reach her destination. She was grateful for her strong legs as they ate up the distance between her and the bus that would carry her away and save her from being caught.

The silhouette of a man standing off to the side of the road brought her to a complete stop.

"Little Bird, you must let me help you before the Dog of Death overtakes you," he called to her.

It was the tribe's Shaman, Shadow Stalker, calling to her in his high, reedy voice. But what did he mean by the Dog of Death? Tricia felt a chill run down her spine as she searched the shadows clinging to the ground around her. She was familiar with her people's odd folk lore and superstitions, usually smirking or laughing at some of the more preposterous ones. But the Dog of Death wasn't one she'd ever heard named before and certainly not by the Medicine Man himself.

She stood still and shouted back.

"Why do you stop me, Shadow Stalker? I haven't seen any dog on the road."

"You are a foolish child, Little Bird. I have seen in my vision that you are running away and I understood your peril. But now, there is a beast roaming these hills that would devour your spirit light."

Tricia peered again into the darkness, trying to make the shadows reveal their secrets.

The Shaman suddenly appeared in front of her. Her heart accelerated until she felt dizzy with fear.

"Do not fear me, foolish girl. I have come to save you. Go! I will stand in your place. Go!"

She took off like a sprinter at the mark. Her feet quickly found their rhythm. Just as she reached the lighted street lamps showing the bus stop shelter, she heard a horrifying scream shatter the silence. A minute later, the Greyhound bus lights illuminated the shelter and the young Indian woman within.

The driver pulled over to the side of the road and Tricia boarded in one long leap. She handed the driver her fare and sat down directly behind him, needing the security of the big man's shoulders to feel less threatened.

She looked out past the pool of light from the bus shelter to the dirt road behind them. The bus moved sluggishly back onto the pavement, moving at like a snail across sandpaper. Tricia feared that whatever the Medicine Man saw out there would catch up with the vehicle before it drifted onto the roadway. She clutched her bag to her chest and sighed in relief as they gained speed.

At last, they hurtled toward the lights of a city, nestled in the distant foothills. This would only be a stop-over for her as she planned long ago to go from that small town all the way to Chicago, a city that had a vibrant art scene.

She settled into the cushions of the bus seat and looked around at some of the other riders. Their faces ghoulishly popped out of the gloom of the bus interior, as lights from on-coming cars shone through the large windows, or riders turned on over-head lights.

She relaxed enough to think about the Shaman, Shadow Stalker. He had warned her that she was being hunted by some kind of evil animal. She wasn't even certain what Dog of Death meant, but the scream she heard riding the night winds still resonated inside her head.

Was the Medicine Man dead? Was she still being hunted by some evil being? *The old one is crazy* she thought defiantly. *How could he know I was going to have to run away? Away from…what I did!* She was tortured by questions without any possible answers, and her head felt like it was in a vise. She rubbed her temples against the developing headache.

Leaning back against the head rest, Tricia closed her eyes, seeing only the shadows of the passing lights upon her eyelids. After a while, her body eased into the rhythmic sound of bus tires on asphalt.

Sleep was not something she welcomed, but after her adrenalin fueled escape to the bus stop, she gave into its allure.

She dreamt of the mysterious and beautiful Black Hills. The rough terrain with its lush color and complex scents was slowly consumed by a heavy, shroud-like mist as she gazed around. Tricia understood. With a sad heart, she realized that she would never return to the land of her ancestors. She was now a renegade.

Her dream took her back to the small room where she left the chilling body of the Reverend Reed. The blood seeping from under his outstretched arms moved like some living entity, moving steadily closer, and closer to her feet.

She ran and ran and ran.

Chapter 3

The bus lurched. Tricia came awake with a jolt. Brakes squealed as if to signal the end of the long, dusty ride.

She looked around herself, anxious, and a bit confused. How could she have let her guard down and fallen into such a deep sleep? Somewhere in her brain, she believed that she could never totally relax again.

Gathering up her bag where it had slipped onto the seat next to her, she got up. Her legs were stiff. She felt shaky and disoriented.

She put the purse over her shoulder and walked down the steps when the driver opened the bus doors.

The Greyhound station was nearly empty. The large clock on the wall read one-fifteen and Tricia had to remind herself that was one-fifteen in the morning. She would normally have been snuggled deep under one of her mother's hand-made quilts. *The mornings at home are very chilly,* she thought randomly as she looked around. Giving herself a mental shake to refocus on the needs at hand, she walked past the empty rows of chairs and up to the ticket window.

The woman behind the heavy, bullet-proof glass merely nodded by way of greeting. Indians weren't high on her list of favorite riders. Even to her bigoted eyes, however, this young woman was clearly not like the transient ones trying to get off the Res, up in the Hills.

"I'd like a ticket to Sioux Falls please."

"Round trip?" the ticket agent asked in a flat, nasal voice.

"N…no. Actually, I was wondering if you could tell me how much a trip to Chicago would cost."

"Which is it? Sioux Falls or Chicago?"

"I don't think I have enough money for a ticket to Chicago, but..."

"It's gonna be a hundred forty to Sioux Falls."

Tricia had less than twelve dollars with her, but she had her mother's debit card. She was given permission earlier that week to use it to pay for more art supplies.

She knew her mom felt guilty that they didn't have the money to help her go to college. Letting her have small purchases seemed to make he feel better.

Up until now, Tricia never abused the privilege.

She reached into her purse and took the card out of its sleeve, studying it for a moment before slipping it through the slot in the thick glass window.

"One way to Chicago, please."

The agent took the card and read the name, looking back at the young woman. She had an anxious look about her, but the agent was too disinterested to wonder why.

She wrote up the receipt and slid the card into the charge reader.

"Have a nice trip," she said mechanically; looking away.

"Oh, by the way, can you tell me about how long it will take to get there?"

The woman sighed with the effort of having to answer.

"About fifteen-plus hours. You'll have lots of time to sleep." With that she turned from the window, signaling she was done being civil to the girl.

Tricia hated using her mother's money, knowing how tight things always were for the family. *At least they won't have me to feed any more* she thought as a defense for her actions. She sat down on one of the hard bucket seat chairs, evaluating her surroundings.

It was small, with dingy gray walls that seemed to bring the misty shadows inside from the darkness surrounding them.

There was only one other person in the waiting area. He stood perfectly still, arms outstretched to either side of a dirty window sill, facing the night outside the airless room.

She judged him to be well over six feet. Even from behind, he seemed to exude a kind of savage machismo that made her shudder deep inside herself.

His shoulders were very broad. It was obvious he was well-muscled under the tight fit of a faded jean jacket. His legs were long and spread eagle, like a soldier at parade rest. Her eyes were drawn downward to his butt, which filled out his tight jeans to perfection.

While she studied him from behind, she tried to catch a glimpse of his face, reflected in the window.

She figured he was Indian, noting the long, black hair streaming down his back. It was tied at the nape of his neck, secured with a thin leather strip.

Her artist's eye was drawn to a small hoop earring in his left ear. It caught the dim light of the waiting room from time to time, glinting like a piece of gold found in a dark pool of water.

Her gaze drifted down to his large hands where they gripped either side of the window sill.

She noted each was covered in distinct and intricate tattooing.

Tricia had a clear view. She recognized at once the dark silhouette of a wolf on the top of his left hand and a burning arrow on the right.

Definitely Indian she thought with a small shudder of fear going through her. While it wasn't odd to find another Indian from the area traveling, she was anxious not to be seen by anyone who might recognize her. She watched the stranger with covert looks now, trying not to get caught doing so. It occurred to her he might have been waiting for someone; someone who didn't show. He seemed to be intensely searching the inky shadows outside the grimy window.

She thought his hands looked very strong, with a square shape that pleased her aesthetic eye. While she was admiring this attribute, he slowly turned and looked directly into her eyes.

"Good morning. It seems I won't be traveling alone after all."

Chapter 4

He had a beautiful smile, with a mouthful of perfect, white teeth, flashing from a sensual mouth.

Tricia smiled back at him, overcoming her usual shyness around strangers. Oddly, he didn't feel unfamiliar to her. Looking into his dark, piercing eyes, she was puzzled to feel they had some kind of connection.

Not at ease with that bizarre notion, Tricia looked away from the tall Indian saying, "I don't know that we have the same destination."

He gave a soft chuckle.

"Oh, I think the next bus in is the only one scheduled for here; and then on to Chicago. I assume that's where you're headed. Unless of course, you just like hanging out at Greyhound Stations at two in the morning."

She looked back at him and saw he was smiling down at her. No use in pretending she had other plans.

"Well, yes. I am going on the Chicago from here. I have family there."

She had to look away from those dark eyes again, so he wouldn't see the lie written all over her face. She'd always been a bad liar.

"Oh, really?" He said softly.

He moved to the set of seats directly across from her and sat down. Leaning back into the hard chair he stretched his long legs out in front. They reached just under the chair next to her. Tricia immediately felt some kind of weird energy flowing around her head. It felt like a swarm of bees had descended on her.

He was still smiling at her in that enigmatic way that was beginning to annoy her.

He knows I just lied about visiting family...I can feel it. Is he laughing at me? But she was tired, too tired to care what a stranger, even one as good looking as this one, thought about her.

"Am I right in thinking you are from the Black Hills Res?"

Tricia knew she could never admit to that. She nervously crossed her legs and looked him in the eye to answer.

"No, I'm only passing through."

"But you are clearly the most beautiful Sioux woman I have ever seen," he said as if to prove his point about her being from the Res.

Tricia wasn't an aggressive girl, but she obviously didn't back down if she felt threatened. She told an even bolder lie.

"I've been living away at school and have no family on the Reservation."

"I see. I'm just passing through this area myself. Chicago is actually my home town. What part of the city are you visiting?"

She tried to deflect his questions by asking one herself. She knew this was a dangerous path to take, but the sound of his voice and his nearness kept her involved in fabricating stories for him.

"What do you do in Chicago?' she asked quickly to ignore the question hanging in the air between them.

"I'm just a struggling artist; trying to keep body and soul together," he answered.

"An artist? Do you paint cityscapes or portraits? What are your subjects?"

He was beaming at her now. He clearly loved talking about his profession.

"It sounds like you know something about art yourself, Miss. Excuse me, I should introduce myself properly. I'm Jackson Wolf. Friends call me Jack. Or if you prefer, Stone Wolf as my people named me.

He smiled when disclosing his Indian name, but Tricia could see he was proud of it and what it signified for him.

He held out his hand as if to shake and she slipped her small hand into his calloused, strong grip.

"Tricia Cooley," she said, drawn into the depth of his stare.

He kept hold of her hand for several heartbeats longer than proper, but she didn't make a move to pull away.

"Tell me your given name," he said.

This was not a request from him, but rather a firm demand that she couldn't refuse to comply with.

"I'm called Little Bird," Tricia replied, but quickly recovered adding, "But only on those rare occasions I see family."

She desperately wanted to distance herself from her tribal name and her own association to anything related to the Black Hills.

She withdrew her hand from his warm clasp, oddly regretting doing so. He continued to smile at her like he had taken something he desired from her without her consent.

"We have a long wait, Tricia. The bus won't arrive until five thirty. There's a twenty-four hour diner just down the road. Will you let me buy us an early breakfast?"

Tricia hadn't eaten since her lunch the day before, the day her life was changed forever. The mention of food stirred her to realize she was weak from hunger as well as stress.

"That would be fine, but I'd like to mention where we're going to the ticket agent in case the bus comes in early."

"You have fine, big-city instincts, Tricia. Always leave something of yourself that can be followed."

She found this a strange remark, but it left an impression on her, a kind of hint for her future actions. It definitely felt like there was a warning wrapped inside his words.

The "Anytime Good Food" diner was situated at the end of the short block, so Tricia could easily see the Greyhound station.

It sat like a squat, lighted mushroom, or perhaps an alien space craft just landed from one of the glowing stars that shot through the velvet black of the night sky.

"This isn't the quality of restaurants we have in Chicago, Tricia, but it will fill us up!" Jack said.

They entered and seated themselves at a booth near the grit-covered front windows. There were only a three other customers, all men, hunched over their mugs of coffee as if receiving a blessing from the steam.

The men were all wearing the rough-looking clothes of laborers, or field hands. There was only one woman present, the waitress. She was standing behind a long gray Formica counter, refilling cups like the attending priestess in a solemn ceremony. There was no conversation between any of workmen. The quiet of the restaurant was only broken by the sounds coming occasionally from the small kitchen at the back, and the waitress blocked the window to a more complete view of the cook. A spatula scraped across a griddle and an intermittent metallic thud of a pot revealed his presence.

"Feels pretty dead in here, doesn't it?" Jack was saying under his breath as he looked around.

Tricia didn't bother answering, but continued to snatch looks around the place, from under her long lashes.

She had an uncomfortable feeling that started the minute they entered the diner. She couldn't pinpoint the origin, but her eyes kept returning to the row of men sitting hunched over and sipping at their mugs.

There was no food in front of any of them, which was probably what the invisible cook was preparing.

The waitress seemed to wake up to their arrival and put the coffee pot on the warmer behind her. She came from behind the counter, grabbing two well-used menus from their holder.

The men at the counter never turned an inquisitive eye toward them.

The waitress looked to be in her early forties. Her hair was the color of dried straw, spun into a perfect, abandoned bird's nest. She had smeared dark blue eye shadow and dark liner around flat, mud-brown eyes, giving herself the bruised look of a battered woman. Her eyebrows came to sharp points, drawn on in heavy black pencil, creating a permanent look of surprise.

Tricia noticed how tall the woman was, maybe close to six feet. Her full figure was squeezed into an ill-fitting uniform. It was heavily marked with the condiments of her trade.

Jack hadn't taken his eyes off the three, unmoving figures at the counter. Tricia began to feel afraid.

The waitress had a name tag on the collar of her stained yellow uniform that read "Margie". Jack gave her a quick look and then refocused on the trio.

Tricia was ready to take the menus being held out to her when Jack spoke.

"Good morning, Margie." The waitress never acknowledged his greeting, instead took out her pad and pen ready to write an order. "Margie, how long have you worked here? What's good on the menu?" he asked, this time watching her response.

She seemed unsure of how to answer, instead asking in a robotic tone of voice, "What do you want to eat?"

Jack kicked out his foot and connected with Tricia. "Give us a minute to decide, Margie," Tricia said quietly.

She was looking at Jack now, and saw he had slipped something out of his jean jacket pocket. It looked long and shiny. "What are you do…?"

Before she could finish her question, Jack had leapt out of the booth and grabbed her arm. He pulled her toward the door. All three men jumped up and were now standing shoulder to shoulder, blocking their escape.

Tricia snatched a look behind them where Margie was still standing by the table, as if they had never pushed past her.

Jack whispering close to her ear, as they faced the three men. "*Shifters*! Get behind me Tricia. When I say run, get out of here and back to the station."

"But the waitress…"

"Is dead!" he hissed back.

She moved behind Jack's broad back, taking a last look at the waitress, still staring off in the distance.

There was a snick sound as Jack released a long blade from its silver handle. He held it close to his side, evaluating the men he called shifters.

The men were all Sioux Indian, likely from one of the four other Reservations west of the Missouri River. None were familiar looking, but they seemed to know Jackson Wolf.

The biggest of the three was looking at her protector and spoke to him in a deep voice.

"I see you Stone Wolf".

Chapter 5

A frightening thought flashed through her head while Tricia watched the three men blocking their escape.

Have the Tribal Police found me already?

Then it occurred to her that it was Jack Wolf they seemed to know. Was he a criminal too?

She didn't have time to speculate any further.

There was a blur of motion. Jackson attacked the man who spoke, driving his long knife deep into his throat. His victim dropped to the floor with a fountain of blood spraying the booths and stools on his way down.

The two other men suddenly produced weapons of their own, some kind of survivalist knives with long, wicked-looking, double-edged blades.

Jack looked each in the eye and spoke in a serious, almost fatherly tone. "Are you certain you want to die today, friends?"

They hesitated, giving each other sidelong looks. Tricia saw one feign a move toward the door, but knew he would charge. The retreating Indian suddenly threw his blade at Jack's hunched form only to have his intended victim snatch it from the air like a Frisbee. Both would-be attackers stared in disbelief for a heartbeat, then turned and fled out the front door. Tricia was too stunned by what she had witnessed to move when the door to the kitchen was suddenly flung open against the wall.

Instead of a chubby, grease-spattered cook standing in the doorway, there was a giant of a man. He wore tight fitting jeans and boots with a black denim shirt opened nearly to the waist showing off a muscular chest. His eyes focused only momentarily on Tricia, but she saw they were like burning red coals. His face seemed ordinary with the exception of those eyes. He was Indian like the others, but she was certain he would not run like they did. This man radiated power and supreme confidence. Only his eyes moved while he studied the tableau of the bloody body, and the two of them. His eyes ignored the waitress, Margie, who stood as if taking their food order, oblivious to life, even her own.

Jack slowly rose from his fighting stance and took Tricia by her elbow, moving her slightly to his left and closer to the front door. As he did so, she distinctly heard him whisper a quick order to her. "Get back to the station. I'll come shortly."

She didn't even know this man, a man she just witnessed killing another like he was slaughtering a pig. Even so, she knew she had to obey his order if she wanted to survive.

She backed away from the scene until she reached the door. Pushing it open she turned to sprint toward the bus terminal.

Before the door shut with a whoosh behind her, she heard a scream not unlike the war hoots practiced by the more aggressive young males in her tribe.

She didn't slow her pace, making it back to the murky confines of the Greyhound station a few minutes later.

The ticket agent looked up, but immediately lost interest, seeing it was just the Indian girl she had waited on earlier. Not prone to chatty conversation, she turned her back to the waiting room and to Tricia.

Panting from her run back, Tricia sought out a seat furthest from the door. She looked around for another exit, spotting a door nearly obscured by the shadows in the back of the room.

Taking a minute to calm herself, she did some deep breathing. She got back to her feet and approached the dirty front window with its view of the street.

Leaning close to the gritty pane, she peered into the cloying darkness.

Suddenly, the bland face of the huge Indian loomed in front of her like a pale red moon.

Tricia screamed, jerking back from the window and the leering face.

With a powerful punch, disregarding the splinters of glass cutting into his fist, he reached for the cringing girl.

His large hand missed Tricia's arm by inches. It was close enough to drive her to the back of the room, toward the rear exit.

She shot a quick glance in the direction of the ticket agent as she ran past. The woman had on earphones, apparently oblivious to the unfolding drama. Tricia didn't stop to explain, exploding out the door into the night. She frantically searched for somewhere to hide from the giant that was coming for her. She saw three large trash containers near the back wall of the terminal and lifted the first lid. It was full to overflowing. Same with the second. The third was empty and she tipped it on its side and crawled in, pulling the lid after her as best she could.

The smell almost made her gag. She pinched off her nose, taking shallow breaths through her mouth. The back door slammed into the wall, sending vibrations through her hiding place. She sensed the big Indian, knowing he stood nearby, silently studying the dark ally.

Without warning, her hiding place was airborne, lifted a few feet from the ground.

She tried to stabilize her body by pushing the flats of her hands hard against the sides of the metal can and wedging her feet against the bottom. The man slammed the can back to the ground, sending the lid skidding into a clump of weeds. The can landed on its side again, rolling up against the building.

Tricia was too terrified to move or scream. Her hands covered her ears, trying to dull the shrill ringing in her head. She remembered the glowing red eyes peering back at her a few minutes earlier. She knew she had looked into the face of a monster.

Growing up on the Res, she never put much store in the old stories of spirits roaming the land, dismissing them as mere folk legends to keep kids well-behaved.

Her mother used to tell her tales of evil men called Skin Walkers, who changed themselves into many animal forms, even taking on the persona of another person.

The Mission school she attended as a little girl was intent on weeding out such beliefs from their young students and made them a topic of ridicule, but her grandmother especially liked to frighten a naughty Tricia with stories of creatures known to her people as Dire Wolves. The terrifying beings of her tales stood close to seven feet, their bodies covered in a coarse black fur. They had the long claws and fangs of a great bear and used these to tear apart their victims in a torrent of blood and flesh.

In her state of near hysteria, Tricia could not rationalize away the monster who would pull her from her hiding place any second. Frozen with fear, barely breathing, she waited to be discovered. There was a scuffling sound like bare feet on the packed dirt behind the bus station. She scooted deeper into the large can.

Dim light from the moon created two large shadows on the ground in front of her hiding place.

Tricia felt her heart leap in her chest when she heard the low rumble of a growl answered by a deeper snarl. She didn't move a muscle as the low, throaty growls became roars. Whatever was out there would do battle and she feared that the winner would take her as its prize.

Chapter 6

Huddled into a near ball, Tricia was no longer aware of the reek from the garbage pail where she hid. All her senses were closed off save her ears and eyes. There was no escape route unless the creatures destroyed one another. A prospect that wasn't likely.

She hadn't seen anything of the second creature, but his shadow. It was enough to realize he was not in human form.

The sounds of their guttural snarls was enough to convince her they were both powerful, well-matched for the battle that raged in the pale moonlight. That silent witness hung almost directly above the alley now, where Tricia waited for a terrible death.

The shadows of the two showed them locked together in a howling embrace. There was an awful snapping of bone. An arc of blood crossed in front of her hiding place, splattering dark drops near the opening of the can.

Complete silence brought Tricia an acute awareness of every breath she took. Her muscles bunched in her legs, ready to propel her in desperate flight.

She crept forward on her hands and knees, the filth of the large can ignored as it covered her hands and clothes. She came close enough to the opening to peer out onto the immediate area.

There, lying in the feeble light of the cloud-shrouded moon was the huge man from the diner. His eyes were wide open, but no longer glowing like red-hot coals. His body was covered in long, deep gashes and looked as if it floated on a pond of blood.

Tricia noted that the man's head was at an impossible angle, his neck clearly broken. Still unable to gather the courage to leave her hiding place, she crouched, stiff with fear, trying to decide what to do next. She began to become aware of a heavy metallic odor wafting over her and hanging like a fog inside the metal can. It forced her to move a fraction more to try to gulp in some fresh air. Her head was beginning to swim in the close confines, but she couldn't exit until she was certain the other monster was gone.

Watching the ground in front of her hiding place, she saw only a single shadow. She sighed in relief as she realized it was definitely a human shape. She poked her head out enough to see who was standing so close to the carnage.

"Jack!"

She sprang out of her metal refuge and threw herself into the arms of the tall man. So desperate to be held, she didn't realize his body was covered in gashes, his clothes slashed and hanging in ribbons.

She pulled away for a second, telling him how the horrible man was really a beast, calling him a Chiye-Tanka, a creature who is a spirit from the woodlands according to Sioux legend.

Tricia hated this character most, of all the ones her grandmother and mother used to subdue her free spirit. To her young mind, he was too human and monstrous at once, confusing her with the easy blurring between the line of natural and unnatural.

As she blurted out her fear that they had encountered this evil being, she drew back further from Jack's embrace.

That's when she saw his wounds and tattered clothing. There were dark stains spreading on the front of his shirt and down his leg. He smiled when she finally took note.

"Guess we both need a bit of cleaning up, Tricia."

"You were the other one in the alley? I thought it was two monsters…but I know I saw the shadow of two…"

He reached for her hand saying "Come on. I know where we need to go first."

They walked down the empty streets until Jack stopped her, pointing to the front of a small store on the corner.

"Let's do some shopping first. You seem to have picked up a strong fragrance of old eggs and coffee grounds and I need to wash up."

He gave her a weak smile.

She started to ask him what had happened, but he held up a hand to silence her.

"I'll explain later."

She closed her mouth, deciding to keep her questions for a better time, but they chased around in her head until she wasn't even sure what she thought she had seen.

They walked behind the store and Jack produced his long knife once more. This time he used it to gain entry to a small clothing store.

Inside, she followed this strange man over to a rack of western style shirts. Jack grabbed one and moved to a rack of jeans.

Tricia wandered over to the section marked *Women's Duds*, finding a black pair of jeans and a white shirt with red embroidery.

She looked around and found some plain white cotton underwear and a bra that looked like something her grams would have worn in her youth, but she made sure to get a larger size than the old one she was wearing. She didn't intend to show it to anyone, so it didn't really matter to her what it looked like. It was clean, and right then, she needed to feel clean. She used a small women's bathroom to wash off as much of the garbage stink as possible.

During the quick sponge bath, it occurred to her she was standing naked with the mysterious man who saved her life only a few feet away. Slipping into the new bra and panties she felt an odd tingle inside as she brought the hooks together behind her back. She reemerged wearing the slim fit black jeans and the crisp white shirt. It felt good to be in clean clothing that actually fit.

Jack was standing in the middle of the store sporting his new clothes. They fit him like a second skin, showing the smooth curve of his biceps and heavy leg muscles as he shifted nervously from boot to boot. She decided she liked the sizes he'd chosen, too.

A deep silence closed out every night noise from the street and surrounding hills as he looked her up and down and then again.

Tricia suddenly felt shy in front of him.

He was studying her very intensely as she nervously ran her hands through her long raven hair. He cleared his throat. "Little Bird," he said, using her chosen name, "search for a pair of good walking boots and socks before we go."

"Why do I need boots? My sneakers are fine."

"We won't be taking the bus from this station, but from the next town over. It's too dangerous for us to travel the route they are aware of now."

"They?" she asked

This was becoming more of a nightmare by the second. Tricia was terrified about the unnamed searchers, but knew they were looking for her.

As they left the shop by the back door, Tricia wondered why this man felt obligated to help her. He'd already saved her in that alley. He could leave her to her own fate, but instead was talking about how they'd make good their escape from, what?

Chapter 7

It was getting close to sunrise as the pair entered the town of Blue Pines, a long seven-mile hike behind them, keeping to the rougher country roads.

Because she walked or ran every day for exercise, Tricia had no difficulty managing the pace set by the long strides of her silent companion.

There was little conversation since leaving the clothing store. She had seen Jack place more than a hundred dollars on the counter while she was slipping on her new boots, his honesty in that act oddly comforting.

"Let's head into the first café we see. I've worked up an appetite and I suspect you've not eaten since leaving home."

She looked down at her watch as they walked down the center of the silent town.

"How do you know we'll find one open? It's not even four-thirty."

"There is always an all-day café in a town the Greyhounds pass through. Just like in the days of the stage coach. Still gotta feed the passengers and water the horses, or fill up with gas."

That was the most Jack had said since they started their odd journey together. Tricia found his voice soothing and his thoughts clearly stated. She looked forward to hearing him talk more, almost as much as she looked forward to her first real meal in over a day.

The *Rise 'N Shine Café* was mid-way down what appeared to be the main street of town. Tricia could smell the bacon and what she hoped was good strong coffee as they approached.

Before they entered, Jack took her hand again, something she was surprised to realize felt comfortable.

"Let me check this place out before you enter, Little Bird."

He seemed to always use her given name whenever he slipped into his serious, or cautious mode. She never called herself by her Indian name unless forced to and wondered why it was natural to hear him address her with it. Another question to tease out an answer to later.

He opened the front door as Tricia leaned against the wall just outside the window. She tried to peer through the glass, hampered somewhat by the fogged up glass, though she noticed people turning at the sound of the front door and Jack's entrance into their early morning world.

She counted four people at the counter, including one very elderly woman wearing bedroom slippers and knee socks. They all had their meals in front of them, busy buttering toast or forking up eggs.

Her eyes spotted a young man sitting alone in a back booth, his sandy colored head bent over the mug he was stirring. He appeared to be smiling at a private joke as he poured more cream into his cup.

Her attention was drawn away by the sound of the front door opening and Jackson motioning her inside.

As the door closed behind them, Tricia saw everyone turn as one to see who had entered. After a few overt stares looking her over, they turned again and resumed sipping, chewing and speaking in low, droning tones.

The young guy in the back booth had lost his far-off look, but was now gazing at the beautiful Indian girl as if she had wings to go with her angelic face.

He laid his spoon on the table and watched as Jackson led her to the booth directly in front of his.

Tricia scooted over on the seat so that her companion would block the unsettling stares directed at her.

She had to admit to herself, he was very good looking, in an all-American, football hero way. She bet herself he had a letter sweater getting moth eaten in a closet at home where he lived with his mom.

She began to relax, letting her mind drift for the first time as she turned the menu over not really reading it.

So many horrible things have happened and I can't go back to change them. Got to get away as far as I can before they find his body.

Jackson hadn't missed the looks the man behind him was giving to Tricia when they came in, but he'd found him to be a non-threat to her.

He was just enamored with her beauty, something Jackson was trying hard not to succumb to himself.

He had wished more than once since this all started, that he'd not been chosen as her protector. She was a temptation and diversion he didn't need in his dangerous life.

The Medicine Man, Shadow Stalker, had called him to his small cabin on the Reservation. "Stone Wolf," the man had insisted, "you will carry out an important task for me and for the good of one of our People. A young woman will be hunted for taking the life of a lecherous fool who will attempt to savage her innocence. You will travel ahead of her when she escapes this dark place and meet with her at the start of her long journey. She will need much protection because this man she killed will be hungrily consumed by the Skin Walkers. Her scent on his body will drive them to hunt her, to claim her and her spirit, as one of their own."

He remembered how Shadow Stalker wheezing slightly after this explanation and stopped to take a deeper breath. "You know the penalty for killing a white man by one of The People. The law will never put into the balance the circumstance of her self-defense. The Skin Walkers are sent by a shadowy figure from my visions. I cannot see his evil face. But I do know for certain that we must save Little Bird before she is taken from us forever."

Jackson was brought back abruptly to the present by a smooth baritone voice. He turned his face and looked up at the deeply tanned stranger from the next booth.

"I apologize for the intrusion, folks. I just wondered if you'd be traveling on the next bus out of this place and knew when it was leaving."

"We haven't been to the station yet. Just came in to get a bite." Jackson answered evenly, though the man was clearly addressing his question to Tricia.

As if on cue, the waitress came over, gently pushing her way in front of the visitor and took their orders.

Tricia was famished and wasn't sure when she'd next get a chance to eat. She ordered the special double everything platter. The good-looking stranger smiled at her as if approving her healthy appetite. His teeth were picture-perfect and when he smiled attractive dimples appeared on either side of his lean, chiseled face. He seemed to know he was handsome as he casually ran a hand through thick, sun lightened, blond hair, almost winking at her in the process.

There was definitely something about the way he looked at her that made her want to have him look at her a little longer. Sort of like getting a compliment and wanting more of the same.

When she heard Jackson clear his throat, she realized she'd been smiling up at the young man and immediately looked down into her mug of coffee. She didn't know why she should feel embarrassed for flirting a little, if that was what she was doing. It seemed that her companion didn't approve.

"I won't keep you from your meals, folks. Thanks anyway."

He started to turn away, but paused and looking at Jackson added, "Hope the hound can out-run the bad weather that's rolling in."

He gave Tricia another brief nod and returned to his booth.

Jackson was uncomfortable sitting with his back to the stranger, but couldn't very well start shifting seats.

He had a prickly feeling creeping up and down his spine. This kid wasn't just a footloose cowboy on the road for the fun of it. He was something else, something that Jackson knew he should recognize but couldn't quite identify.

He leaned forward enough so Tricia could hear him and whispered.

"Eat quickly, Little Bird. We need to leave soon."

Tricia looked back at Jackson with a question reflected in the narrowing of her dark eyes.

"Just enjoy your food and we'll talk later."

He drank deeply from his cooling mug, glancing out the fogged-up window at the gray light tinging the edges of the coming dawn.

Their meals were delivered a few minutes later and eaten in silence.

Tricia could feel the eyes of the stranger on her whenever Jackson moved and unblocked his view.

He smiled once when she caught him watching her, but not before she saw a more serious look pass over his face.

Wonder why he looked at me like that...like he knew something about me wasn't right.

She was distracted from her meal momentarily, wondering if there had been some kind of news article about the killing and naming her as a suspect.

Jackson reached across and tapped her arm.

"Ready to leave, Tricia?"

"I'd like to use their facility first," she answered looking over at the sign for the restrooms.

She had to pass the dimpled stranger who was trying hard not to be obvious as he watched her walk by. She noticed he hadn't eaten, but was putting money on the table for his coffee and seemed ready to leave himself.

After washing her hands, Tricia studied herself in a small square mirror hanging over the sink. She looked better since eating, but there were dark smudges under her eyes from lack of sleep. She'd try to do that on this long bus trip.

It was odd, but she felt comfortable with the idea of sleeping in Jackson's company. His protectiveness made her feel safe. He'd proven his ability to defend her back in the other town. She brushed out her long hair until it streamed like a shimmering black veil down her back. Tricia was glad she never left home without her small make-up bag. She put on a touch of light eye shadow and tried to cover the dark circles under her eyes with a touch of concealer.

Thinking of home stirred a sob from deep within her. Home was now out of her life forever. She had no home, no family she could turn to, no life back on the Res.

She stared at her reflection and quietly murmured, "You will become a new person. Tricia Cooley will no longer be Little Bird."

She turned away from her reflection, and taking a deep breath walked toward an unknown future among strangers.

Chapter 8

Jackson noticed the faint touch of make-up Tricia had applied and thought she looked more beautiful, if that was possible. He appreciated the fact that she needed little artifice to enhance her natural beauty. Feeling irritated with himself for even noticing her exotic face and voluptuous body, he turned it on her and snapped, "We need to leave now, Tricia. That cowboy left here five minutes ago, but he's bound to be hanging out at the bus terminal. I hope you didn't get spruced up for *his* sake!"

His voice had a hard edge to it that confused her.

Tricia mumbled something about trying to look more human and pushed past him and out of the café. Now she was a bit prickly herself thanks to his attitude.

After five minutes of irritated silence while they headed toward the Greyhound station, Tricia finally blurted out what she'd been thinking. "I never said you had to help me in any way you know. You just appointed yourself my guardian or something!"

"You are a very foolish girl, Little Bird. There is much you are unaware of and I don't have the time to explain. But let's be clear on one thing; I am here to keep you safe. If I am self-appointed, does that really matter?"

She looked up at him, not answering. She couldn't deny wanting to be near him for safety and something else, something she wasn't sure how to identify yet.

Jackson walked quickly, with sure, long steps, forcing Tricia to nearly jog to keep up.

His mouth was set into a hard line, but the finely shaped high cheek bones and perfect straight nose diminished any unflattering effect. Tricia found herself watching him with side glances. He had plainly said he would keep her safe and that meant the world to her just then. She reached forward, taking his incredibly large hand in her small one. Tricia enjoyed the warmth of his skin wrapped around her hand like a rough, but comfortable wool mitten in winter.

He stopped and looked down at her. The tightness around his mouth and eyes was suddenly relaxed.

"Jack, I'm sorry. I'm certain I owe you my life. Please, forgive me for being so thoughtless. I didn't mean to seem ungrateful. I am truly happy to be taking this trip with you and I don't know what I would do now if you got angry and left me."

He took in the glow of the sun as it rose and was reflected in the depth of her dark eyes. Suddenly, he understood. She had placed some kind of magical spell over him from the first time he looked into the depths of her gentle, doe-like eyes. He knew beyond a doubt, she had ruined him for loving any other woman. "I'm not angry with you, Tricia. Please, believe that," he said softly.

He reached out his free hand and slowly let his fingers memorize the soft contours of her face. When he came to her lips, he traced their fullness with his finger and then abruptly let his hand drop.

"We'd better get going, Little Bird. I'm not sure when that bus gets in, but we'll need tickets to ride!"

They both smiled at that obvious comment and resumed their walk, still holding hands. It felt as natural as breathing. A few minutes later, they entered the station and immediately sensed an undercurrent in the room. Looking around Jackson realized there was a buzz among the few waiting passengers.

"Hey, aren't you that Injun wrassler from the WWA?" an older man shouted out as they headed toward the ticket agent.

There was a plug of chewing tobacco tucked inside a stubble covered cheek. He casually shifted it to the other cheek, waiting for an answer. A drop of brownish drool escaped from the corner of his mouth. He was sitting with two other men, all looking like typical rough-living ranch hands, out for a good time. They all wore faded blue jeans, plaid snap button shirts and sturdy cowboy boots, caked in dried mud, or cattle manure, probably both.

Jackson looked down on the trio, sizing them up. He knew men like this could be found anywhere on the planet. Some guys just have to pick a fight to prove their own virility and prowess. This bunch looked about right to fit that bill of idiots.

"I think you're confusing me with a different man," Jackson said as he passed by, still holding Tricia's hand.

"That there sweet lookin' female your *squaw,* Injun?"

The man speaking was sitting next to the first cowpoke. There was a smile curling his chapped lips. It never made it up to the blank eyes, staring out of his wind-burned face. His voice was high, reedy, like it should have come from a little man, not the brute laughing at what he thought was quite amusing.

Tricia was immediately on guard and ready to run at the first sign of trouble.

Jackson leaned down to her ear saying, "It's alright. I've got this."

He let go of her hand after directing her to purchase the tickets from the man behind the glass window. He turned his back on the trio, fishing out three-hundred dollars from his shirt pocket. Smiling to keep her calm, he slipped the money into her hand.

The three men continued tossing out suggestive comments and insults. Only when he sensed them standing and coming at him from behind, did Jackson spin around.

He stood very still. His muscles tensed with a surge of blood that came with his aroused anger and rush of adrenalin.

All three men stopped where they stood, giving one another sidelong looks as if trying to appraise their companion's fighting ability.

Their faces were twisted, looking like a pack of snarling dogs, yet each waited for the other to make a move.

Jackson had seen their kind and fought their kind. Now would be no different.

He spun around on one foot like a whirly dervish and struck the nearest man full in the face with the heel of his boot, breaking his nose with a loud crunching sound while reducing his mouth to a bloody pulp. Teeth flew from the gaping red mess and the man fell to the floor followed by the echo of his cry of pain.

The man that had first spoken to Jackson and the remaining thug separated, getting some distance between them. They would attack Jackson from front and back.

Jack watched the older man approach slowly.

The ticket agent had just completed giving their tickets to Tricia when the fight began. He had been oblivious to the taunts and threats of the three white men and assumed the Indian had started the altercation.

"Hey, you take that outside, ya hear me!" he shouted impotently through his bullet-proof glass enclosure.

Tricia clutched the tickets to her chest and watched as Jackson methodically turned the remaining two men into chopped meat. There was blood everywhere along with several more teeth and at least one set of dentures.

Tricia ran over to him and pulled him away from the scene.

"The bus won't be here for at least two more hours he told me" she said nodding in the direction of the ticket agent.

"Let's get out of here and catch it up the road."

Tricia nodded toward the front door. She was anxious to leave the station and the bloody scene before some law showed up.

Jackson was still pumped, but let himself be led away. They immediately began another long walk to the next stop, another fifteen miles down the road according to the Greyhound Schedule tucked into Tricia's satchel.

"Guess they were just itching for a fight" Jackson said between breaths as they walked fast.

"And you sure gave them something to scratch!"

They were hoping the bus driver wouldn't realize they were the couple involved in the mayhem back at the station. He'd likely stop for them even before reaching the next official stop. Out here, folks did that for you.

The three rough men had dragged themselves out of the building and were piling into a vintage station wagon with wood-paneled sides, headed for the nearest walk-in clinic. Luckily, this meant they wouldn't be around to help explain the fracas.

Only one other person knew what had happened in the small terminal since the agent was not sure exactly what he'd seen. This man sat quietly in the deepest shadows of the waiting room, close to the back door where he had slipped in unnoticed before the fight broke out.

He smiled to himself and ran his hand through his thick blond hair. "Guess we'll catch up later, Stone Wolf," he whispered into the darkness.

Chapter 9

They heard the sound of a big engine echo off the sides of the surrounding hills as they made their way out of the small town. A beat-up Ford pick-up pulled over to the side of the road in front of them a few minutes later.

The weather-beaten face of an old Indian was smiling back from the driver's side.

"You two need a ride?" he shouted.

"Come on, Tricia. This could be our lucky day after all." Running up to the truck, Jackson pulled the door to the front seat open and motioned for Tricia to climb in. After he followed suit the driver gave each of them a grin.

"Welcome my brother and sister. You are going to be riding in the oldest truck in all of South Dakota, with possibly the oldest driver, too!" He chuckled and looked over at his passengers. "My name is Thomas One Tree and I am still trying to figure out where the rest of the forest is."

They all laughed at this amusing remark, likely made upon every introduction over his long lifetime.

"I'm Jack Wolf, Thomas, and this is my friend, Tricia Cooley. We appreciate your stopping for us."

"Nice to meet you both. How long is your road?"

"We're going to the next Greyhound station in Peeking Rock, a few towns over," Jackson answered.

Jackson felt there was something familiar about this old one, but then, most old Indians he came across had the same kind of aura, born of much experience with being Indian in a culture driven by white capitalism. It seemed to soften them around the edges, like fast-moving water over hard stones.

"Ah, I know that station. My grandson left from there four years ago when he joined the Army." The old man grew pensive for a moment, gnarled hands gripping the wheel tighter. "He never did come back home, that boy. Vanished like a drop in the ocean." He shrugged at his loss, then went on to tell them the Greyhound Station was about an hour and a half off, over the back roads they would be traveling. "I'm going that way anyway folks, happy to have your company."

Tricia had felt a twinge of sadness for the Elder, for surely he was an Elder in his clan. He seemed very sharp in spite of his apparent age and his manner implied someone used to advising and leading. She had gotten a good look at him as he drove, taking quick glances whenever they spoke. Thomas was apparently enjoying the attention of such a lovely young woman and he chatted away with her about his life as a small rancher not far from her own home on the Res, a fact she was careful not to reveal.

When he questioned who her own people were, she almost panicked, but Jackson saved her an explanation by offering to drive them until they got to the terminal.

"Ayo that would be very good of you. I admit I've been on this dusty road for several hours now and missed my afternoon nap."

Without waiting for further discussion, Thomas pulled the truck over to the side of the road, trading seats with Jackson. It took a minute longer to get everyone resettled and Jackson had them back on the road. The old man was asleep before they'd gone a mile and Tricia scooted closer to Jack to give him more room.

He gave her a brief smile when she shifted closer. She became very aware of his scent, earthy and sensuous. It teased her nose and made her squirm a little on the cracked leather seat. She realized his nearness was arousing some primal need in her, something that started deep in her body.

Jackson kept both his hands tightly wrapped around the steering wheel. He knew if he didn't, he'd be grabbing this beautiful girl entrusted to his care and pulling her into his arms. He gave his head a sharp shake, like a dog shedding water.

"Are you OK, Jack? I can take over driving if you want."

"I'm fine, Tricia. Just need to loosen up."

The old Indian had dropped his head onto his bony chest. His blue veined-hands were clasped together and dangled between his scrawny legs.

Jackson looked over at him and whispered down to Tricia.

"Sleeps like an innocent babe. Makes me happy we came along to give him a little break."

Tricia was beginning to feel the effects of her harrowing escapes and flights as a fugitive.

She watched the road as the old truck slowly rattled over hills and down into empty valleys. It became a mesmerizing experience and her eyelids began to falter and close. She tried to force them open, but finally gave into her exhaustion, falling into a deep sleep.

Her head drifted over and soon was bouncing as it lay on Jackson's shoulder. He took one hand off the wheel, gently maneuvering her onto his chest. Laying his arm around her, he pulled her closer, to keep her in place.

Jackson looked down every few minutes at the sleeping beauty. Tricia had pulled her long hair into a pony tail earlier and it felt silky under his hand. He could feel her warm breath on his chest where her mouth lay close to his shirt. It was almost too much for him.

He began to feel angry with himself for allowing himself to feel so deeply attracted to this young woman. He was to be her protector, not her lover. Or was he?

As he held Tricia close to his chest, he began to feel as if someone was watching him. The truck was quiet, save for the throaty rumble of the laboring engine and the tires on the rough road.

He shot a quick look over at Thomas One Tree. Though his head was now resting against the window, Thomas had turned it toward the driver. He was smiling warmly, deepening the lines and creases that marked his face with age, like the rings on a tree.

"You have been awake a long time, Thomas." It wasn't a question. Jackson felt the old man had been watching him.

"I have been awake. I clearly see your affection for Little Bird grows with every mile we travel. Please, do not be ashamed of such a pure emotion as yours in front of me."

Jackson took note that Thomas had used Tricia's Given Name when it hadn't been spoken earlier.

"You speak like a wise man, Thomas. Perhaps you have slightly misled us with your simple manner," Jackson said, looking over at him when he said this.

"Thomas One Tree is every bit as simple a man as you have seen. I am a bit more complicated, Stone Wolf."

Jackson pushed down on the brake, lurching them onto the berm of the road. The truck jerked to a stop. He tightened his grip on Tricia and she woke with a start.

"What happened? Why have we stopped?" she said looking around the cab of the truck and out the front window.

They were sitting on the side of the road and she knew they hadn't arrived at the Bus Terminal.

"I think I fell asleep," she said sheepishly.

"You needed to sleep young lady," the old man said with a grandfatherly smile.

"I will be leaving you both here, as I have traveled as far as I needed."

Jackson just stared at the old Indian. "What?" Tricia asked. "You're leaving us… and your truck? You can't be serious. We only wanted a ride…not to steal your truck! Jack, tell him!"

Thomas had already opened his door and looking back at the two inside said, "Stone Wolf will explain to you, one day, Little Bird. You have need of this vehicle while I no longer do. It is my gift to help you down your path."

He walked around the front of the truck, both Jackson and Tricia closely watching.

When he got to the driver's window Jackson looked down at his upturned face.

"You have been watching us this whole trip."

"It is what I do, remember that. You must hurry now. Your way out of here is just down the road a few more miles. Carry out your duty to me, Stone Wolf, and be rewarded with this girl's freedom and happiness."

"Where is he going?" Tricia was shouting, trying to watch the retreating back of the old man as he climbed a small hill covered in scrub grasses and disappeared behind several large boulders.

"No, you can't let him walk away, Jack!" she yelled as she jumped from the idling truck.

Jackson leapt down to grab her around the waist and haul her back.

"It's alright! I promise you, it's alright!" he kept repeating.

Tricia was being dragged back toward the truck when they both saw a lone wolf dart out from behind a scattering of large rocks. It was silvery gray and very large. Its long legs carried it quickly into a fringe of wooded area and it was gone.

Chapter 10

"Why would you let him leave us like that, Jack? He'll die out there all alone! That wolf might hunt him because he's easy prey. He'll be killed and you could have stopped him!"

She was furious with him for letting the old man leave and take off on his own. It didn't make any sense to her. Why would he abandon his truck to strangers anyway? And that wolf would surely find him without any protection.

Jackson knew he had to share some of his secret with her. She would not cooperate in her own rescue if he didn't give her a reason to be afraid.

"Tricia, please, let me explain some things to you that will help you understand why I let Thomas One Tree leave us so unexpectedly. I know you are upset with me, but there is a reason and I think it's time you knew more about your circumstances."

She had settled back into the front seat of the truck, but sat as far away from Jack as she could. The handle of the door pressing into her side reminded her she could jump out anytime if need be.

Her arms were crossed tightly across her waist, causing Jack to be distracted with the excited rise and fall of her breasts under the thin white blouse.

He looked away for a second and when he looked back he had a stony expression fixed on his chiseled features. The tawny bronze of his skin and determined set of his jaw made him look like a noble warrior she'd tried to paint in her art classes.

That brought a sharp jab of memory of the body lying in a pool of blood.

She shuddered and looked away and out the windshield until his deep voice brought her back to his face.

"Tricia, I am of The People, but my clan is separate and has been since long before the time the white man intruded his road into our lands. I, like my father and his father, back to history that is not recorded but only remembered by our Shamans, have been initiated into this small army called Keepers. Our one task is to protect the People of the Tribal Nations from the evil that walks among them."

He was speaking in a soft, but convincing tone, like a historian giving an important lecture in Native American History. Tricia became riveted to his narrative, unconsciously leaning in toward him, to catch every nuance of his words.

"In the dawn of its formation, the Keepers fell into serious and destructive discord among their elite group. There was a secretive war conducted between those who wanted to use their powers to protect our peoples and those who chose to use this power as a weapon for their own evil ends.

This splintering of the Keepers resulted in a band of renegades that many have come to know as Shape Shifters."

He stopped speaking when he heard Tricia's sharp intake of breath. This was going to scare her as it would any sensible person, but there was no easy way to tell a story about monsters.

His features softened as he saw her face reflect the fear, deep rooted in the tribes and peoples of many in the Indian nations. "The shadowy myths of Shape Shifters, or Skin Walkers as some people know them, passed over many cultural barriers and lands like storm clouds across the sun. Many among the People sneered at any Shaman who warned of Shifters walking among them, or called them superstitious fools. These were mostly the young tribe members; the only warning they heed now is from the ring of their cell phones."

Jackson reached over and gently placed his hand on Tricia's arm. "Please understand, Little Bird, I am here to protect you from any harm. I need to explain these things to you so you'll cooperate for your own good."

Tricia didn't move away from his touch and in fact, relaxed under the pressure of his strong hand.

"Please, tell me why I am being hunted, Jack. I have had that feeling now since…"

"Since you ran away from your would-be attacker."

"How..."

"It was known to Shadow Stalker, the Medicine man of your clan. It was seen by him in his vision, as was your innocence. Tricia, you were defending yourself against a would-be rapist and it makes no difference to his guilt that he was white."

She was feeling lightheaded with the shock of her secret being revealed by someone she barely knew. She leaned forward slightly to bring the blood to her head and help the dizziness.

The next thing she knew, she was lying against a gently rising and falling chest, Jackson's chest. The smell of his body and the feel of strong arms wrapped securely around her shoulders was both comforting and exciting.

She must have passed out. How else had she come to be held in his arms? She didn't want to move and break this ring of strength that surrounded her. And there was something else, a stirring deep within her body that woke and grew as his breathing stirred the strands of hair on her face.

Tricia wanted more than anything to feel this man's hands on her body and his mouth pressing hard on hers. It was ridiculous to feel sexually aroused at a time when her life was being threatened, but her body didn't care.

He must have felt her stir because he gently lifted her face until she was gazing into his searching eyes.

"Are you feeling better, Tricia?"

"Yes. I think I must have fainted because of lack of sleep, or food, or…"

"Because of the story I'm telling you?"

He pulled her closer to his face and she found herself looking at his slightly open mouth.

In the next breath his lips were crushing into the soft pillows of her own. They parted, and his tongue searched her hot, wet mouth with impatient jabs and thrusts. His hand caressed her through the thin fabric of her blouse and cupped her right breast firmly, squeezing and kneading.

Just as suddenly as he began Jackson pulled back and gently pushed her away. He flung open the truck door and jumped out as if escaping. He walked toward a pile of large boulders and stood facing the empty land where the old man and the wolf had disappeared earlier.

Tricia was too stunned by his rejection to move for a minute, but slowly began to rearrange her blouse and run her fingers through her hair. She needed to speak to him and let him know his behavior was something she wanted, welcomed even. Slipping from the truck, she approached him. His back was stiff, unyielding, and unwelcoming.

She reached out to touch his shoulder when they both heard a high-pitched scream. Tricia had never heard such a hideous sound, but she instinctively knew it was the last sound of someone, or something, about to die.

Chapter 11

"Get back in the truck!" he yelled as he grabbed her elbow and helped her scoot through his open door.

"Wait, Jack! Could that have been the old one? We need to help him!"

"That was no human cry, Tricia. Trust me, the old one has taken care of one of our stalkers and that was his warning for us to move."

Tricia braced herself, her hands white-knuckling the dash. Jackson tore away, the tires spiting dirt and gravel until he got back on the road.

She looked straight ahead, wondering how that decrepit old Indian could have defeated a mouse, let alone a wolf.

Was that truly a wolf? she wondered, as Jackson picked up as much speed as the old truck could muster. They flew down the empty road way.

After ten minutes of silence between them, she noticed his grip on the wheel relax. The truck slowed. She had glanced at the speedometer earlier and it read seventy-five. She didn't think the truck capable of even fifty for any length of time.

"Jack, I need some explanation of what's been going on. First that creature coming after me back at the diner, and then the bus station and now, this! You need to tell me who or *what* is hunting me."

She stared at his strong profile, waiting for answers. It was her life that was being threatened and she was totally in the dark. If she weren't so scared, she would be angry.

"You deserve to understand the nature of this threat hanging over you, Tricia. Just let me get us to the next town and somewhere we can breathe and I'll give you your answers."

He glanced over at her, and Tricia nodded her head before leaning back into the cracked leather cushions.

They arrived at a non-descript small town with the unlikely name of Big Bend, quickly locating the ubiquitous Greyhound station. Jackson said it was two stops after the original station. "I know we beat the bus here and according to the ticket guy, we have another hour to wait," Jackson informed her while she paced nervously by the front window. "Let's get some coffee at the shop next door and then we'll talk."

Moving through the waiting room, Jackson caused heads to turn and eyes to follow among many of the female passengers waiting on a bus. He was as graceful as a dancer and with his good looks, even Tricia found herself stealing covert looks at him as he walked.

They brought their cups of steaming coffee back to the bus terminal so they could be first to board. Sitting close together in the plastic bucket seats, they turned their bodies so they were knee to knee, facing one another.

"I'm ready to hear what you have to tell me, Jack," Tricia said with the steel of determination in her voice.

I can't rightly deny her knowledge about her own life, especially since the truth threatens like a dark thundercloud overhead. Jackson took a thoughtful sip from the super-sized Styrofoam cup. "I've already told you a little, Tricia. Your Medicine man, Shadow Stalker, had a dream and saw what happened at the Community Center. He knew you had escaped, but in his vision he also saw a Shape Shifter coming toward the building, onto the scent of blood.

He had taken the form of a kind of mutant wolf and he was searching out easy prey."

Jackson stopped speaking for a second when he realized Tricia was beginning to tremble. He put his cup on the floor and took her hand in his until she seemed to calm down. "You aren't alone, Tricia. Shadow Stalker is a powerful Shaman. As it is, he saw me in that same vision. He reached out to claim my services as a sworn Keeper of The People and sent me on this journey to protect you."

"Tell me more about The Keepers," she said, looking more than a little confused about the secret organization to which he referred.

"In the beginning, when The People were placed here by the Great One, all the clans lived in peace. Among our leaders were powerful Medicine Men who formed an alliance with other powerful Shamans. They named themselves The Keepers. Their purpose was to guard The People from evil forces known to lurk in the world of men. There followed a long history of peace, until they became aware of a growing evil among some of The Keepers. There was a lust sprouting deep in their hearts, a desire to dominate the other clans through dark forces. They were eventually discovered in their shifted form of twisted man-wolf, after they murdered their clan chief and his entire family. As if they were slaughtered sheep instead of loved and respected leaders of The People, they were devouring their kill."

He studied Tricia's face, gauging her reaction. She watched him closely, as if searching for any trace of the shadowy beast she had seen fighting in that alley.

"In their wisdom, and in great dread, the remaining clans formed a band of special *Guardians*. I am part of that group and by that membership have been given access to the strong powers of the old ones."

He moved so he could put his arm around her shoulders. She relaxed back into the circle of protection and he continued. "The Shifter that is stalking you has eaten of the flesh of the white man you killed in self-defense. If he hadn't smelled the blood, you could easily have been his victim instead. The Shaman, Shadow Stalker, knew that once he scavenged the flesh of the dead man, he would become aware through his dark powers how he died and who killed him. Your essence became imprinted on the evil being, absorbed by him. This included the violence of the act of rape and the death of the white man by your hand. The same sick urge to violate you and possess you are now a part of the Shape Shifter's own twisted desires and to a lesser degree, his pack, because they too savaged what was left of the preacher's remains."

"Are you saying I am being hunted by this creature so that he can finish what the white man started back at the Center?"

"That and more. The Shifter doesn't want you dead any more than your attacker did. He wants to own you, body and soul, and bring you back with him as his initiate and then, his mate. Shadow Stalker watched in his vision, as the beast devoured the flesh, along with the twisted desire for you that the dead man held in his black soul. He is now as obsessed with making you his, as the sick bastard that tried to rape you was!"

"But how can I keep running like this? When will I get to start my life over and not be afraid?"

"We get on this bus to Chicago and put time and space between us and him. I am appointed to guard you until you don't have need of me any longer."

"Will there ever be a time like that?"

"I would like you to always need me, but in a different sense," he said softly, without thinking and before he could catch himself. He leaned forward, instinctively, and for a moment he thought she was going to raise her face to get closer, to kiss him, but then they heard the call for all passengers going on the Chicago and they both moved back.

The long silver bus had pulled in front of the station and people were gathering up their belongings for the fourteen-hour trip ahead. Jackson and Tricia had no baggage save her large saddle bag purse stuffed with snacks they had purchased for the road until they could get real food along the way, so they were first to board.

She knew she'd never recognize the Shape Shifter, but couldn't fight the paranoid urge to look for him. Jack's story, for that's what it sounded like though she knew in the pit of her stomach it was true, terrified her. Tricia resisted the urge to cling to him and instead focused on the faces of boarding passengers.

After what felt like an interminable ten minute wait, the large doors on the bus made a swooshing sound and snapped shut behind the last rider. Tricia sensed Jackson's alertness in the stiffness of his body, his large hands splayed on his thighs ready for action. He sat that way until they pulled away from the station.

He had explained some of the mystery surrounding her being stalked by a beast-man, but she had never been a big believer in the tribe's folk tales. Now, suddenly, she was supposed to believe they were true. She just couldn't wrap her head around his story. She tried to sort through the tale of Hunters and Keepers and now his role as Guardian, but once the adrenaline began to wear off, she gave in instead to sleep and drifted into her own shadowy dreams.

Chapter 12

Tricia jolted awake.

"Just a twenty-minute break," Jackson said softly.

She glanced out the window at the rest area. Sitting to long made her feel stiff, and she welcomed a respite from the confines of their seats.

Jackson reminded her they were still on high alert until they could make it to Chicago where they could melt into the millions of faces. She nodded as they entered the visitor center. Inside the sterile building, they each headed for the rest rooms.

Tricia was quick to relieve herself and then spent several minutes trying to touch up her make-up and brush through the tangles sleeping had caused in her hair.

After another inspection in the mirror, she decided she'd done all she could to look less like a weary traveler. Besides, no amount of touching up could cover the fear she saw in her own eyes. *When will all this end? My parents must know by now what has happened to the pastor. His wife surely must hate me.* She had to stop that line of thought or she'd never be able to live with herself. After adjusting her large purse on her shoulder she exited the bathroom and found Jackson waiting in front of the small restaurant with three or four tables.

He was holding two white lunch bags and handed her one as she came up to him.

"Got this for the road, breakfast sandwiches. Hope that's alright for you."

Along with the bags, he indicated the coffees on the table behind him and grabbed one for himself. "Better get back to the bus. We wouldn't want to be stranded here at this fine dining establishment."

They made their way back to their original seats like everyone else was doing and Tricia was able to study her fellow passengers more closely. There was an older couple wearing matching T-shirts. His read, *I Belong To Her*, and hers read, *And Don't You Forget It!* She smiled to herself and watched one or two others enter the dimly-lit bus. It was getting close to sunset and the lights switched on automatically for the riders.

She had seen most of the passengers as they exited the bus earlier and then again at the fast food restaurant. They all seemed familiar now and she was about to look away as the last one boarded just in front of the driver. He was also familiar to her, but not from this bus trip. He shot a quick look in her direction and locked eyes with her.

She stiffened and Jackson immediately followed her gaze to the tall, good-looking man taking a seat two rows ahead of them on the left.

"Do you know him?" Jackson whispered close to her ear.

"I...I'm not sure. He just caught my eye and I got a funny feeling before I could look away."

Jackson was drilling holes in the back of the man's head now, trying to sense any danger from him. His own common sense told him it couldn't be anyone from the last bus terminal, or he would have seen him when they first boarded the bus, almost four hours ago.

He tried to study the guy who sat across the aisle from his position, and was able to examine his profile when he turned his head to look to the right. The guy was likely in his early thirties. He had the sculpted features found in any of the Hollywood hunks stalked by paparazzi and crazy girls. His hair was an ash blond and Jackson could tell even from where he sat, that he had a real tan, the dark color proclaiming him to be a true outdoorsman. Even as young as he appeared, he had the tell-tale fine lines of someone who spent hours squinting in hot sun.

Cowboy on a local ranch? Jackson wondered. He tried to place the man since he obviously had some kind of unsettling effect on Tricia. Jackson noticed he wore jeans, faded with many washings. When the stranger stretched out his long legs into the aisle, he saw the well-made boots with intricate embossing peeking out from under his jeans as he crossed his feet at the ankles. *Now, those cost a few dollars. Owner of a big ranch?*

The man had on the common plaid, snap-front shirt of the area. His arms were so well-muscled the fabric around his biceps threatened to tear open at the seam whenever he moved and flexed his muscles. His neck was as thick as a weight lifters, yet there was a definite grace about his smallest movements.

While he'd been studying the young man as best he could, something about the way the subject was sitting struck Jackson. He looked relaxed, with his legs outstretched, one immense forearm lying on the seat arm, but there was a tautness in his body, like he was ready to spring up at any moment.

The passenger sitting next to the cowboy had gotten to his feet. Jackson was distracted for a second by the elderly Indian that stood looking apologetically at the cowboy.

"Need to use the bathroom, young man," he was saying loud enough for those around him to hear, including Jackson.

The handsome stranger immediately got to his feet to let him pass into the aisle. He smiled courteously at the old man and then looked directly into Jackson's surprised face. So intent on his scrutiny of the cowboy, as he'd come to think of him, Jackson was surprised to suddenly be staring into the glint of his cold blue eyes.

Tricia turned from watching the countryside fly past just in time to see the brief connection between the two men. Though the face was only vaguely familiar, the build and the eyes were the same as the man they'd met at the Rise & Shine Café. *But that was hours ago and he didn't board with us*, she thought distractedly.

The old man shuffled past their seats on his way to the tiny restroom. In passing, his hand slipped casually off the seat backs he'd been using for support and grabbed Jackson's shoulder.

"So sorry, young man," he said apologizing. "Just a little unsteady on my feet."

Jackson was about to speak when the old man squeezed his shoulder tightly as a father would a son upon greeting him. He was smiling as he passed and Jackson had to suppress his own smile in return.

The cowboy had retaken his seat, but seemed pensively waiting for his seat-mate to return. He leaned forward slightly watching out the window from time to time.

Jackson studied the back of the cowboy's head. *You must sense something, don't you cowboy? Something powerful is riding with you.* Jackson Wolf did smile this time when the old man passed his seat, again touching his shoulder. Jack reached up to touch the gnarled, but firm hand for a second, as he called the old man's name under his breath, "Thomas One Tree."

Chapter 13

Tricia missed the interaction between the old Indian and Jack, but her sharp hearing picked up the name *Thomas One Tree*. Her head snapped in his direction. Leaning closer to him she asked, "Did you just call that old Indian, "Thomas One Tree"?

Jack reached for her hand where it lay on his arm and squeezed it gently. "The wise one has sent another Guardian Keeper to our aid. I suspected as much back in the truck with the old one, but now I'm certain." He turned his head to look her in the eyes. "You and I both know who the cowboy is sitting next to him, Tricia, and he's probably following us…you…and has no idea he's sitting next to a Keeper."

Jackson felt a little more relaxed knowing the true identity of the old man as a Guardian Keeper. While the Medicine Man, Shadow Stalker, had given this Protector assignment to Stone Wolf, he wasn't surprised he also sent the old one as back up. Tricia had no idea of the evil she had unwittingly called down upon her life back on the Res. Shadow Stalker must have known this evil would test him as her Protector.

Wrapped in the monotonous hum of the bus tires skimming the road, Jackson found he was more than a little aroused sitting so close to her body. He inhaled the floral fragrance of a body cream she must have used at one point, perhaps before her life became this running nightmare.

Giving her a sidelong glance, he saw she had closed her eyes, her head resting against the window. The occasional lights from passing trucks winked like fireflies off the black curtain of hair cascading down her shoulder.

Jack had to fight the urge to reach out and encircle her with his arm, knowing she'd awaken. They hadn't spoken about the incident in the truck where they both gave into their mutual desire for one another. This wasn't the time.

Stopping for the next scheduled rest area, Jack looked up to see the cowboy standing and stretching in the aisle. He leaned over to tell the old man they had stopped for a twenty-minute break.

"I'm going to buy myself a sandwich for a late supper. Can I bring you anything back?" he asked loudly so his seat-mate could hear him over the chatter from riders preparing to get off the bus.

The old man must have mumbled his reply because the cowboy touched his forehead in a quick salute and exited the bus. Jackson looked over at Tricia's sleeping form and decided he'd take the opportunity to connect with the old Indian.

"Good evening, Old Father." He greeted him respectfully, knowing full-well this was an ancient Keeper and deserving of this ritual greeting. He sat down next to the frail looking man.

"Stone Wolf, you are as I am, not one to sleep as others, until the hour is darkest. How goes the journey with our Little Bird?"

Jackson had been careful to make sure they were the only people on the bus besides the sleeping girl, so they could speak freely. He answered carefully so the old Keeper would understand all was under control, but his presence was greatly appreciated. "It goes well enough old one, but there have been encounters along the road. And if your presence is any indication, there will likely be many others."

The old man chuckled into his narrow chest, the deeply seamed face looking like a shriveled winter apple. His head seemed more sparsely covered with gray hairs than it did in his guise of their earlier meeting. Even his body appeared to have diminished in size, making him appear frail and doddering. Jackson suspected this was a great way to present himself to any potential adversary as they'd immediately underestimate his power and hidden strengths.

"Will you be going on to the city of Chicago, old brother?"

"Oh, yes. My own mission is clear enough and you shall be in need of my particular aid when the time comes."

"What of this cowboy sitting next to you? Is he a threat to me as a Keeper?"

"Not to you in that role, Stone Wolf. But in another, he will most surely be your rival."

He began to make that wheezing chuckle into his chest again and as Jackson was about to question him further, other passengers began to trickle back on board for the last leg of the trip. They'd stop only twice more for new passengers to board.

Jackson returned to his seat and the sleeping beauty he longed to kiss, but instead, he took off the jacket he'd been wearing to slip it around her slender shoulders. He watched her gentle breathing and felt reassured that she was resting well. He reached up and turned both over-head reading lights off. By the time they were all back on board, the rider sat in semi-darkness, except for the usual cell phone glow from various points.

The cowboy brought back a hamburger and fries for the old Indian. Jackson felt a small twinge of annoyance, thinking this was merely an ingratiating gesture. The blond man casually rose to remove his jacket and shot a quick look in Jackson's direction. His smile seemed sincere, which made Jackson even less happy. It wasn't good to like your adversary!

Chapter 14

The old man's voice rose enough for Jackson and Tricia to hear him say, "I'll just wait till everyone is off, young man. No sense in keeping all the other people waiting for my old legs to start working." He chuckled.

He looked rested to Jackson's eyes, but probably had never slept a wink over the entire trip. This old Indian was truly a powerful Keeper, he thought with a smile. Jackson and Tricia had both exited the bus, passing the blond cowboy as he stood looking down at the elderly Indian.

The bus had picked up a handful of passengers at the last rest stop to make the last leg of the journey into Chicago. Two men and a middle-aged woman had boarded around five in the morning, each carrying breakfast burritos and heading for the back of the bus. The men looked almost identical in their features and were likely brothers or maybe twins. The woman seemed related, probably by marriage, to one of them. Jack heard her directing which seat she preferred, as they passed him.

Tricia had been awake for an hour by the time they picked up the trio. Jack noticed her watching them pass with a guarded interest. As soon as they were out of earshot, he leaned closer. "Anyone interesting in that group?"

"Oh, no. Just seem to watch everyone lately."

They'd been discussing the old one and the cowboy since she woke up. She confided that the cowboy didn't scare her, but she knew he was the same man that spoke to them briefly in the diner the day before.

"Why wouldn't he say something about meeting us then?" she wondered.

"Likely didn't want us to think he'd been following us, Tricia. He looked back at me though and he knows I recognize him."

Tricia seemed fidgety, moving around in her seat until finally she said, "I need to get up for a bit. I'll use the restroom and be right back."

Jack figured she probably wanted to scope out the trio in back. He had to admit, there was something flat about the vibes they were giving off when they passed close to him earlier.

He turned to look behind him just in time to see the woman approaching the small bathroom at the back of the bus. The three companions had taken the last seats running the length of the bus, giving themselves a view of all the passengers. Nothing unusual about that, but Jackson studied the woman closer as she griped the cushioned back of an unoccupied seat. The hand was so large it immediately caught his attention. His eyesight was perfect and he was able to see the dark hairs covering the knuckles where she held onto the seat back.

His gaze moved upward on her arm and he saw the well-defined bicep that only a body builder would sport, unlikely in most females. Her long-sleeved knit shirt couldn't hide the bulge of muscle. Jackson was certain he was looking at a man and concerned that he hadn't picked up on this sooner. Tricia was several rows behind him and he needed to get back there without drawing attention to himself. He was certain the imposter would attack her the minute she opened the narrow door. With his focus on the back of the bus, Jackson hadn't been aware that the old Indian man was standing a foot away.

Acting like he was using Jackson's seat for support on his way back to the restroom, he bent his wiry frame toward Jackson's ear.

"I think you should let me get this, friend. They'll react to you if you approach them now and the girl will walk into a hornet's nest." He chuckled as if they had shared a private joke. Before he could gather himself to make a response, the old man became a blur of motion, a ripple in the dimness. The nodding passengers wouldn't be able to discern his movements in the dark interior of the bus.

Jackson sprang to his feet, facing the back rows. The narrow bathroom door opened and he saw Tricia reach back to shut off the dim light. As Tricia started down the aisle, she was met by the elderly Indian. He smiled in a grandfatherly way as he stepped in front of what appeared to be three sleeping riders.

"Evening, miss. I'm just waiting my turn. Thanks for not being long."

Tricia felt warmed by his gentleness and answered his warm smile with one of her own. She saw something in the old one's eyes that gave her comfort and she didn't want to break their visual connection. They stood in that friendly pose until Jackson broke into their locked gaze.

"Tricia, if you are ready to sit, I need to speak with our friend here for a minute."

He'd all but told her to get back to her seat and Tricia was annoyed at his assuming he had authority over her. She looked between the two men and decided she'd rather search the darkness for a black cat then try to understand males.

When they saw she was reseated, the old man gave Jackson a friendly grin before speaking. "As you know, these three are all sent by their Master to track Little Bird's movements. I've put them into a sleep they shall never return from. You can get her safely off this old bus when we arrive in Chicago."

"I thank you, old one, for this intervention. I know our Shaman, Shadow Stalker, has been watching us."

Jackson let his attention wander back down to the three strangers lined up on the back row, looking like targets in a shooting gallery. The *woman* had taken on a blueish coloring, looking like she should have been on a medical gurney rather than a bus.

"What did you do to them?" he asked. He could not control his curiosity and even awe that this frail-looking man had defeated three Hunters singlehandedly.

The elder smirked and said, "My specialty."

He unsnapped his shirt pocket and pulled out an oval shaped piece of wood. Jackson recognized it as a power talisman, similar to those used by his shaman. This was a carved eye, the size of a fifty cent piece, its pupil colored a deep red and outlined in black.

The grizzled hand swept over each of the three bodies, carefully pressing the eye to each forehead. The bodies trembled and one by one, they disappeared.

He tossed the wood chip over to Jackson who caught it mid-air, turning it over in his hand to study. "They are only as strong as their spirit projections and if you interrupt that, they are nothing but air. The eye is yours if you like. I don't really need it."

Jackson knew there was more to this explanation. Many of the older Keepers had been trained in the more arcane secrets of power and were reluctant to share this knowledge. One day Shadow Stalker would impart more of the ancient powers to him, preparing him to take over his role as shaman.

"Who's sending them?" Jackson asked, his voice tight with anger and apprehension.

"Well, I don't rightly know yet, young Keeper," he whispered back, his voice a rasp like steel wool on an iron pot.

Jackson was now convinced this man was one of the elusive Black Feathers, mavericks from among the ranks of the Keepers. They performed their services only when pressed by the Shaman to use their enormous powers. Otherwise, they were a reclusive group, small in number.

"But as sure as the Great Spirit guards The People, the truth of who they follow shall come to light for you, Stone Wolf." The old Indian studied Jackson's tightly composed face in the dancing lights from the oncoming traffic. "By the way, the cowboy sitting next to me is called Bryce Powers. He is also known as Dancer. Can't tell you more, I'm afraid. But I sense your unrest with his presence. Remain guarded, young wolf."

His face took on a deadly serious look when he made his last comment.

As he returned slowly to his seat, Jackson noticed that all his fellow passengers were nodding off, or sleeping. It seemed strange that an entire busload of folks would all sleep at the same time. The old one's face sprang to mind and he knew the answer to that mystery at least.

He was thinking about this as he passed the last of the dozing riders and sat down next to Tricia. She was looking out the window, but he knew she was annoyed at him for telling her what to do earlier. Her body was stiff with her irritation. The reflection of her beautiful face, currently set it firm lines, brows slightly furrowed, confirmed his observation.

"Little Bird, forgive me if I seem too bossy to you at times. I am not trying to be, but it's important you listen to me, if I am to keep you safe. It's an area in which I've developed some expertise. You have to trust my experience and judgement in such things, or you might endanger us both."

She didn't turn to face him until he stopped speaking and then she met his dark eyes and caught her breath. She dropped her gaze momentarily, looking back up with a small smile that made his heart skip a beat. "I'm sorry too, Jack. I shouldn't be so touchy. Guess my feelings are confused right now." She reached over and squeezed his hand where it lay along his thigh. He swallowed, forcing himself to remain still rather than turning his hand to capture hers.

Just then, the cowboy passed down the aisle and leaned over to speak to Jackson. "We'll be there in another half-hour. I can be reached here if you all need a guide around Chi Town." He held out a piece of paper and Jackson automatically took it from his hand. Giving Tricia a nod, he returned to his seat next to the old man.

Jackson watched the arrogant cowboy stride with athletic agility back down the aisle toward his seat.

Looking at the note, Tricia read an odd message in a barely audible voice. "Be seeing you soon." Below the scrawled message was the name, Bryce Powers. Jackson took the note from her hand, mumbling something under his breath. A shock of intuition ran through Tricia. The handsome stranger somehow knew they were running from someone, or something.

Who are you Bryce Powers? she wondered as the bus left the highway, rolling down big city streets lit up like an arcade as they approached their final destination. Could she finally end her running here, just another face among the millions? And what of these two men she was so drawn to? How would they fit into her life? Should she be afraid of them, or trust them?

She stared out the streaked window of the bus and realized she'd been holding Jack's hand when she felt him turn his large hand to grasp her smaller, more delicate one with his strong, capable fingers. She looked over to find him studying her face in the subtle light of a waking city.

"Don't be afraid, Little Bird," he said as if reading her thoughts. "I will keep you safe until you can fly the skies of your dreams without fear."

Chapter 15

It only took them a few minutes to get out of the Greyhound Terminal. They had no luggage to collect like the other passengers. Tricia noticed Bryce Powers had also exited the bus and went directly through to the front door of the station. She watched as he turned left on the sidewalk in front and disappeared from view.

Still looking toward the front door she felt Jackson take her elbow and gently guide her through the milling crowds and outside.

"Tricia, I think the first order of business is to find apartment. We both need a good long shower and rest. Then we'll go out and eat and learn a little about your new home."

"Is this just to be my new home, Jack? Are you planning on returning to the Res soon?"

"I've told you, Tricia, I am here as your Protector and will be here as long as you are in need of my services as a Keeper."

That seemed to quell the panic he had seen in her eyes when she asked if he'd be going away. He felt a stab of guilt that it made him happy to see her fear at the thought of his leaving. He gave himself a mental shake for being so selfish, but he knew he couldn't leave Tricia until she asked him to.

"Where will we look at apartments, Jack? I don't have the money for the first month's rent."

Jack had taken her hand as he crossed the street in front of the Terminal and headed toward a cigar store where he knew he could pick up a newspaper.

"Just let me handle the particulars of the rent, Tricia. Money is not a problem right now."

She looked over at him and he knew she was skeptical of that statement, but she went along without voicing any doubts.

They stepped into a gloomy, narrow shop in an old building. It was crammed with merchandise, taking advantage of the limited space. The air was dense with the smell of cigar smoke and pipe tobacco.

Inside, Jackson motioned for her to wait by the store front while he went to speak with a man standing at the back, likely the owner or manager, judging by his age.

"Morning," Jackson greeted him as he approached the cluttered counter.

He reached for the morning newspaper and casually asked about any apartments he might know of for rent around the area.

The man looked up at the large Indian looming over him, standing momentarily with his mouth hanging open. Then, reverting quickly to big city shop keeper, he shook off his surprise and took up the business of making a living.

"Well, this must be ya lucky day fella. It just so happens, my brother moved out ta California for his health, and I'm tryin' to rent his place out…dirt cheap, I might add."

"Where is the apartment located and do you have someone to show it to us?"

The store keeper shot a look over Tricia. The rising sun was stronger now and Jackson noticed how it showed off her slim but curvy body, nicely.

"Sure, I can get my nephew to come down here for a minute so I can show it to you and the lady."

With that, he picked up the phone and spoke to someone on the other end, saying "Get your fat butt down here, kid. I wanna show the place."

Jackson had no intention of living above this shop, especially if this guy owned the apartment. He saw him checking out Tricia like a fine steak and knew that could mean trouble.

"We want to grab a bite to eat, so we'll be back in an hour so there's no rush." He tucked the paper under his arm after throwing down two dollars. He moved away from the counter as the man was cradling the phone and took Tricia by the hand. "See you later and thanks."

The shop keeper knew a blow off when he was on the receiving end of one and called after Jackson's retreating back. "Hey, not everyone is willin' to rent ta Indians ya know…better remember that."

"Guess that didn't go too well, but now that I have a paper we can check rentals ourselves."

Jackson was relieved when Tricia didn't object to not returning to the cigar shop.

"That man was crude and kind of scary, Jack. I'm glad we're going to look elsewhere."

After a walk that helped them both unkink after the long bus trip, they ended up having a great lunch at a little Italian place off the Loop. Over Veal Parmigiana, he told Tricia a little more about himself, hoping to allay any fear she had about sleeping arrangements once they found a place.

Jackson related how he'd been to Chicago once before, for an extended investigation into a run-away from the Res. It was his job to find the kid, a fifteen-year-old boy, and bring him home. There were rumors on the street where the boy was reportedly seen, that he had been taken forcibly into the sex trade.

Jackson admitted he felt depressed for months by his failure to carry out that assignment and relieve the family of their greatest fears.

Tricia saw the pain he carried, echoed in his eyes as he talked.

To his mind, Jackson viewed big cities like he would someone with bubonic plague, best to avoid both!

With a mixture of humility and pride Jackson described his place in the elite band of Guardian Keepers, after Tricia asked more about that secret band. He told her he was considered one of the most powerful and clean of spirit among the Keepers and had a grandson's relationship with the Shaman, Shadow Stalker.

"I've already told you, it was Shadow Stalker who sent me on this mission, Little Bird."

They finished their meal, lapsing into a relaxed silence. Jackson let his mind wander back to when he met with his most glaring failure to protect one of The People. He felt the weight of the bad memory strengthening his resolve to protect Tricia against the Hunters.

Looking up from his drained coffee cup, Jackson said, "If you're done, Tricia, let's start checking out some of the apartments listed for rent."

They both got refills and Jackson slipped the waitress a twenty-dollar tip, making sure they would be undisturbed as they searched the paper.

There were three apartments listed within a five mile radius according to the map of Chicago they had between them. The waitress had given it to them after ripping it out of a battered phone book.

"Jack, according to this map, the Art Institute is several blocks from here."

She'd split the pages with him and had been concentrating on the area closest to the famous Art Institute of Chicago, a place she only dreamed of ever seeing.

"We can grab a cab over to that neighborhood and look around. How many apartments did we circle in that area?"

They left the restaurant twenty minutes later and began to walk the nine blocks. Tricia couldn't stand the thought of having anything but her own feet under her after the seemingly endless road trip.

Along the way, they stopped to look around themselves at the buildings and into shop windows. The crowds of people seemed endless, but it dawned on Tricia it was now Friday afternoon.

"Jack, I think we'll have to buy some clothes first thing after we find a place. I feel so grungy wearing the same things for two days."

He chuckled a little at that comment, thinking the same thing applied to himself.

"Let's get the apartment and then we'll shop. Promise."

Although she worried about the money, Jackson seemed fine with covering their expenses. She hoped she could find some kind of work so she wouldn't need to rely on him so much. *I have to take care of myself, or I'll never survive here after he leaves,* she thought.

She looked longingly at the beautiful clothes displayed on impossibly thin mannequins. She unconsciously smiled, knowing her own body was more voluptuous. She visualized the tight tops and skirts clinging to her soft curves and full breasts and felt something new stir inside herself, a feeling of sexual power.

Observing her reflection in the glass, she now understood what she saw in the Pastor's eyes, naked lust. She was desirable and men were affected by her, even to the point of some kind of insanity.

She studied the Tricia in the glass. Since she had the tools to get all she needed in life, she needed to be smart enough to use them carefully. She felt something inside herself harden and knew it was her resolve to survive on her own terms.

Chapter 16

They were both getting tired of walking around the crowded, noisy city. Tricia knew Chicago was called the *Windy City,* and after nearly two hours of being buffeted by its gritty winds, she felt even more worn-out, and mistakenly thought the weather was the reason for the city's nickname.

Nothing seemed to bother her companion. He barely took notice of the frequent looks he got from some of the business women pushing past them. He was handsome enough to garner more than a second look in most cases. Even several men gave him a long look as if he was some celebrity on the prowl.

She didn't realize that while she noted all the females giving Jackson a lustful or dreamy look, he was noting the males doing the same to her. Unlike Tricia, however, he was on his guard against male predators, knowing there were some serious Hunters on her trail that would eat these city Romeos as a snack.

They had seen two of the apartments circled in their paper, located fairly close to one another. Both had some problems that Jackson knew Tricia couldn't and wouldn't live with. They had to step over a drugged-out looking man sprawled across the stairs leading to the first apartment. There was angry shouting and screaming coming from the apartment next door to the second one they looked at.

With one left, Tricia was getting worried. "Jack, what will we do if we can't find a place today? It's starting to get late."

"Don't worry, I have that covered. We'll go over to the Drake Hotel. I stayed there for a week when I was here that first time."

Tricia was more than a little curious about the money Jack seemed to spend freely. She stopped walking, a look of serious concern on her face. "OK. I have to know something and it's not because I'm not grateful for all you've done for me. You're spending lots of money and I have no idea when, or if, I can ever repay you, or the Shaman, if it's his money! Should I be worried about where your money is coming from, Jack?"

Jackson looked down at the lovely and innocent face of the young woman. Even her openness was beautiful to him. Before he answered, he took her in his arms and gave her a tight hug, oblivious of the people detouring around the roadblock they made. "Little Bird, don't worry any longer about the money. My small clan are all beneficiaries of a sale of oil rights many years ago. There is no shortage of money because there are only a few of us left to share it.

Shadow Stalker is the oldest among us and when he dies, his share passes to me,

his adopted grandson. I'll have two shares then."

"Oh," was the best Tricia could say to this important information.

The relief on her face confirmed that it had finally dawned on her that Jackson was not only her Protector, but would make certain she was provided for when she was finally settled in her Chicago home.

They turned onto a side street off Michigan.

"Jack, I need you to understand. I want to find work and support myself here. I know I can do that and I want to do that! I don't want you to think your only place here is as a Protector. I...I want you to stay as long as you want to."

Jackson stopped and studied Tricia's serious face for a second before speaking.

"I can only stay for as long as you need me Little Bird. You should understand that Shadow Stalker may call me back to the Res. As a Keeper of the People, I am sworn to carry out any mission my grandfather sends me on."

He saw the fear flash across her face again and hastily added, "I will not be called while you are still in danger, Tricia. And when that has passed, you will be strong enough to face your new life, with, or without Stone Wolf."

They were looking into each other's eyes when the front door to the apartment building opened up and a very pretty African American girl stepped out onto the sidewalk.

She gave them a quick glance and smile as she moved around them.

"Excuse me, Miss?" Jackson said hurriedly.

"Are you a resident in this apartment complex? We were interested in looking at the vacancy here."

"Oh, sure. There's one open directly across from mine, 3C. It's been vacant for over a month," she said, a dazzling white smile highlighting the rich color of her skin.

Tricia felt drawn to this open, friendly girl and asked if she'd mind answering a few questions about the place.

"Oh, no problem. I have off today and was only going over to the coffee shop for a bagel. Ask away. And by the way, my name is Angie."

After five minutes of preliminary questioning, Angie, suggested she take them to meet the landlord. He had the whole of the downstairs for him and his *weirdo wife* as she was described.

Following her into a beautifully refurbished marble foyer, Tricia and Jackson waited while their new acquaintance rang the bell at Apartment 1A.

When the door opened Tricia instinctively smiled at the short, round man wearing house slippers and a Mickey Mouse T shirt over stripped PJ bottoms. She had a quick glimpse of someone, likely his wife, who poked a head of frizzy blond hair around the corner of a front room and then disappeared from view.

"Hey Harold! Sorry to bother you, but I wanted to…"

"Yeah…it's my cartoon day and Joyce won't pause it for me so I'll be missing some."

"Right! Well this is Jack and his lady Tricia. They want to see the open apartment across from mine. Mind if I show it to them?"

"Nah. Here ya go."

He reached behind him and grabbed a set of keys off a key board and handed them to Angie. Without another word, he shut the door in their faces.

The fully furnished apartment had one bedroom, a fairly spacious living room/kitchen, a black and white tiled bathroom with a claw-footed tub with shower attachment. The shower curtain had been thrown out probably as the metal rod hung naked in a semi-circle around the somewhat pitted tub.

Tricia poked around the rooms, noting the bedroom had a view of a nearby park and she was sold.

"Jack," she sidled up to him as he was looking into a storage closet by the front door. "I love it! You can see a park from the bedroom and it all looks freshly painted."

"How much are they asking a month, Angie, do you know?"

"It's the same as mine because we're kinda' like twins…nine-fifty."

"Could we dare to bother Harold once again, Angie? I think we're ready to sign the rental agreement."

Angie went down the stairs like a gazelle, followed by the handsome couple.

She'd been struck by Tricia's beauty and natural friendliness. It seemed odd to her, but the hunky looking Jack seemed more like her bodyguard than her boyfriend. Her discerning eye saw an undeniable chemistry between the two.

"Go away!" Harold yelled from somewhere in his apartment.

"Don't worry guys. Harold loves me and he'll settle down once he knows you want his apartment."

She gave the door another hard knock smiling at them over her shoulder.

The whole process of paperwork and cash down took twenty minutes and Tricia was handed the keys to her apartment.

When they invited Angie to go to a late dinner with them, she gladly accepted and steered them to an Indian restaurant, famous for their Tandoori Chicken on Clark Street.

They ate, laughed about Harold and his *Blondie* as he called her and Angie filled them in on some of the quirks of their new home.

At some point, Jackson asked why the apartment had been vacant for so long in the city.

"Kind of unheard of in a city like Chicago I'd think," he added skeptically.

"Could be because of the murder." Angie said blithely wiping her sticky fingers on the linen napkin.

"What murder?" Tricia blurted out before Jackson could ask.

"Oh, the guy who lived in your apartment was found murdered nearly two months ago. Drug bust gone south I heard. He was some kinda' private detective, or something, the paper said. Nice guy, actually. Kept to himself, but I guess that was because of his work. I helped Harold clean his apartment out and we must have found fifteen small statues of wolves in the place. Must have had a thing for them."

Jackson had been listening intently to her story and when she mentioned the wolf collection, he asked if any were missing their heads.

"Geeze! How the heck could you know that? You must be psychic or something! He had a small box in the dresser that had about six heads in it I think. I just figured he planned to glue them back on."

She looked at each of them intently, fork half-way to her mouth.

"Oh, there is one kinda' weird thing about you guys renting his place. He was Native American too. When I asked what tribe, he said Lakota, or maybe he said Dakota, you know like North Dakota?"

No more was said about the wolves, the murder, or anything other than possible places to find work. It was obvious that Angie regretted telling the story about the other Indian, because her new friends had become very subdued.

"You guys will need to get some food and household items. How about I borrow my boyfriend's car tomorrow and I'll take you to a co-op store I belong to?"

Walking back to the apartment after thanking Angie for all her help, neither one spoke of the murdered Indian man that had once lived and died there.

They silently climbed the worn wooden stairs to where Tricia longed to find some rest while Jackson believed he'd been led into another Keeper's den.

Chapter 17

Tricia found a set of clean sheets had been placed on the bare mattress with a note on top of them.

"Welcome to Harold and Blondie's home for a boundless future. Return clean please."

Tricia sniffed the soft pile and the fragrance of lavender reminded her of her mom, who used sachets of lavender in her closets at home. She wiped away the tears that sprang suddenly to her eyes and returned to the living room.

Jackson was near the large window where he'd shut the blinds against the darkness that had fallen. He looked over at her and smiled.

"Want help making the bed?"

"Sure."

While they each worked on the lumpy looking mattress, Jackson broke their silence.

"Tricia, I have a strong feeling about the guy who rented this place before us. He might have been the Keeper sent before me. His name was Joseph Rain Cloud, Joey Banks in the white world.

He was on another Protector's assignment. According to Shadow Stalker, he decided not to return to The People. He started some kind of Private Detective agency here instead."

"Didn't you contact him when you were here searching for the runaway boy?"

"He never responded to my calls. I just let it drop. Figured he'd assimilated and didn't want to hang out with his clan any longer. Besides, if he was involved in an investigation, having a guy like me around might have drawn unwanted attention to his undercover work."

Tricia looked at Jackson's muscular arms and realized he did look like some kind of enforcer.

"Jack, don't you think the chances of us renting the same place are pretty remote?"

"Nothing about the Keepers is typical of the happenings in the real world, Tricia. I believe we were sent in this direction, to this place, for a reason."

After several minutes of both of them thinking about those possibilities, Tricia stood back from the made bed.

"I think I'd like to take my shower now, Jack, if you wouldn't mind waiting for yours."

There were clean towels in the bathroom with the same note attached to them. She couldn't wait to get the grime of three days travel and walking off her body.

"Take your time, Tricia. I'll be out here."

She saw him slip something out of his pocket that looked like some kind of wooden talisman. She forgot about it immediately when she walked into the yellow glow from the bathroom light and turned on the water for a hot bath.

Thirty minutes later, hair washed as best she could with the bar of soap she had slipped into her purse from the last café they ate in, Tricia felt human again. She pulled her comb through her long hair and tried to study her face through the fog of the medicine cabinet mirror. When she went to put her few but precious make-up items in it, she found a tube of half used toothpaste. Grateful that she wouldn't have to go without some sort of brushing, she put some on her finger and scrubbed her teeth as much as she could. She left the tube out so Jackson would find it too.

She opened the bathroom door and stepped around the corner into the bedroom and called to him.

"Bathroom's free."

A minute later he was running the water and lathering up with the soap she'd left in plain sight. He toweled off and used the toothpaste, wondering if that was in her huge purse too.

With the towel wrapped around his hips, Jackson walked past the bedroom in time to see Tricia standing naked near the bed, putting some kind of cream on her legs. She must not have been aware he was out of the bathroom. He studied her naked body in the soft light of the small table lamp. He couldn't see her face since her dark hair cascaded down her arm and shoulder. His breath caught in his throat as he watched her graceful movements. She had turned her back to him now and was bending over to brush out her hair, probably trying to dry it before bed. Her buttocks were round and firm and her long legs firm and shapely.

She felt herself being watched and spun around.

Jackson was so mesmerized by her movements, he was caught staring into her dark eyes with his desire clear on his face.

Rather than scream out in surprise or anger at his watching her, Tricia quietly placed her brush on the night stand and turned the bed covers down. She didn't try to hide her nakedness from Jack's hungry eyes, but rather was relishing the effect she was having on this Indian warrior. She looked down and saw the towel he was gripping at his narrow hips stir with his obvious arousal.

She got into the bed, never breaking eye contact with him. Jackson dropped his towel on the floor near the bed and followed her invitation onto the cool sheets. His hands were gentler than she would have guessed, as he touched and fondled and caressed her slowly; watching for signs of what pleasured her most. He entered her only after her body became insistent and when he did, it was slow and calculated, every thrust met by her own.

They made love twice more that night, and only slept as a weak light made its way through the gauzy curtains.

Chapter 18

Their new friend arrived at their door as promised, early the next morning.

"Hey guys! Ready for a trip to the market?"

"Let's get some coffee along the way, Angie. Both Tricia and I haven't been made civilized yet!"

They were chatting and laughing like old friends as they climbed into the double-parked Fiat. Jackson could barely fit his long frame into the front seat, while Tricia scrunched up a bit in the back.

Angie seemed happy for their company and drove like she owned the road.

"You are a practiced city driver I see, Angie," Jackson said with some awe in his voice as she narrowly missed taking off the bumper of the car she was passing.

After nearly two hours of gathering food and household items, the trio was filling the car with the purchases when a long, sleek limousine pulled up beside the Fiat.

The three watched as the tinted rear window was lowered. Two startling blue eyes peering from a chiseled movie-star face came into view.

"Well, howdy to you two. I see you've already made a friend in the Windy City! We passed you on Michigan as my driver was taking me back from breakfast and I wanted to see how you were settling in."

Both Jackson and Tricia looked surprised. How did the cowboy that had taken a Greyhound bus from god knew where, to Chicago, suddenly have a chauffeured limo driving him to breakfast?

"How are you, Miss? Enjoying the sites I expect." He addressed his comment to Tricia.

Angie was clearing her throat, making enough noise in the background to be noticed by all.

Finally, Jackson said, "This is our neighbor, Angie. Don't really remember yours," he said pointedly.

The handsome, blond-headed man smiled easily at the slight and ignored the snide tone in Jack's voice.

"My name is Bryce Powers, Miss Angie. So glad to make your acquaintance."

Turning his attention back to Tricia and Jackson he said, "Say, I have a great way for you two to make some other friends in this town. I'm having some other folks new to this area over to my place for a quiet evening tomorrow. A little food, some good whisky and lots of time to meet folks like yourselves, new to these parts. The house is located a good drive away, more countrified you might say. I'd purely love having the three of you join us."

Without waiting for anyone to answer, he reached out of the window and handed Tricia a card. Out of reflex, she took it from his large hand.

"You can Google me and find out some particulars about me, before you come over. Bet you'll be surprised. By the way, I like to hunt too, Jack. See you at eight."

The window went up, concealing the passenger behind the heavily tinted glass.

No one saw Bryce Powers as he smiled to himself and put his fingers to his nose for a long sniff. He had touched her hand when he handed her his card and even in that casual physical contact, he could smell her, almost taste her.

The car made a smooth exit out of the parking lot and back into the flow of traffic. Tricia watched it move like a shark in the ocean, sure and swift and deadly.

She gave an involuntary shudder which did not escape Jackson's notice.

He moved closer to her and taking her hand in his, he raised it to his mouth and kissed her palm. Angie looked on and sighed as if she was at a romantic movie.

"Hey," she said excitedly, "do ya think Bryce would mind if I brought my boyfriend along tomorrow night? Besides, I want you to meet him, Thaddeus, but everyone calls him Teddy." She went on talking about the next evening's party invitation and was oblivious to the quiet that greeted every enthusiastic comment.

One thing did capture their attention. Angie mentioned that the cowboy looked an awful lot like the famous photographer who went by one name. "He was named one of the *Most Eligible Bachelors* in the latest *Chi Town Buzz* Magazine." Studying the card that Tricia passed to her, she speculated out loud, "I think it was something like…Prancer?" She couldn't remember, but said cheerfully, "If it's him, I'll remember before tomorrow!"

Chapter 19

"We *both* need clothes, Jack!"

Tricia had been harassing Jackson for the past hour and looked determined. He let himself be pulled into the large department store.

People were openly staring or turning to look as they passed. The beautiful Native American couple even drew a few comments, as if they were celebrities. Angie loved the attention they were drawing to their little group.

Tricia pointed Jackson in the direction of the men's department and she happily entered the magic world of women's fashions a minute later with Angie at her side.

Angie picked out an armful of items for her to try on. She was continually amazed at how everything looked like it had been designed to show off her body to the best advantage.

Jackson had made it clear, "Buy a wardrobe ladies! Don't hold back on cost."

"My lord, this is so much fun, Trish," Angie enthused at one point.

They had sent Angie back for the Fiat, quickly filled to overflowing with their earlier purchases and Jackson's new clothes and shoes. Tricia's new wardrobe had to be stuffed into a taxi.

"You are ready to meet the world, girl!" Angie yelled out her window as she merged into traffic to drive back to the apartment.

In the back seat of the cab, Jackson took Tricia's hand and squeezing it gently asked, "Are you pleased with your new things, Little Bird?"

She grinned broadly, reaching up to kiss his cheek. "I'll show you all of my treasures when we get home."

Jackson leaned his head back on the seat and smiled to himself. He had never experienced the thrill he just did when she spoke the word home and knew she meant his home too, the one he shared with her.

Angie was already unloading his things when they pulled up behind her on the street. After ten minutes of shifting bags and boxes from the vehicles to the apartment, the couple were left alone to get it all sorted and put away.

Tricia insisted he go back out to the local grocery store and pick up a nice bottle of wine to thank Angie for all her efforts and help.

"Wasn't that pair of shoes we bought for her enough of a thanks?" He clearly wanted to be near this woman and not chasing down a Merlot for their friend.

When he was gone, Tricia began hanging all the dresses, tops, sweaters and other garments in the closet. Shoes, six pair, were neatly lined up on the floor beneath the nearly groaning rack.

They had picked up new toiletries for each of them and she was placing Jackson's in the bathroom in the small dresser they got for such things when she heard a sound coming from the front room.

"Jack? You're back so soo…"

"Hello, Little Bird."

Bryce Powers smiled down into her startled face. He moved toward her and she unconsciously took a step back.

"No need to be afraid. I just came by to give you directions to my place for tomorrow's party."

"How did you get in here, Bryce? Wait…how could you know my given name? Who are you?"

"Well, to answer the first question, I knocked and the door must not have been closed tight, so I came in. As for your Indian name, I must have heard Jack use it sometime along the road."

"Why were you riding a bus anyway? You obviously have enough money to have your own driver," she said moving further away from him.

"I am a free-lance photographer, Tricia. I was taking pictures of everyone on that last trip, you included."

"Me? I never saw you taking pictures. What will you do with them?"

Bryce had slowly been herding her like a lost calf, moving her inevitably toward the bedroom. He had been watching her hanging her new clothes and organizing her shoes carefully beneath. Her fluid movements accentuated the form of her body and once, when she bent over to retrieve a slipped blouse, he had to fight back the urge to run over and throw her onto the invitingly empty bed.

"I will use some in my next gallery exhibit, but yours…well, yours I'd like to use in a top fashion magazine spread. Truthfully, I wanted to speak with you about doing a modeling job for me."

"What kind of fashion magazine? You mean like Elle?"

She was unable to hide her immediate interest and excitement at the prospect of being a fashion model. That life would be so glamorous after nineteen years of living where she could barely get mail, let alone a glossy magazine.

He had come within touching distance of her now, but she was oblivious of that fact while he described a high end industry magazine called *Chanteuse*. He was saying how her face and figure were a perfect complement to a spread he was doing on fashions of the west in America, the focus of the article.

"It's going to be a ten page spread with at least that many pictures of the model on every page."

Tricia was about to speak when the door opened and Jackson was filling the doorway with his large frame.

"What are you doing here, Powers?" he asked with an edge of anger in his voice.

"He came to give me the directions for tomorrow night, Jack."

"And to speak with Tricia about taking a modeling job for a magazine I'm working for right now. Suppose you know by now I'm a fashion photographer. It seems Miss Angie recognized me earlier."

Tricia was looking between the two men. They were puffed up like two bull frogs. She found them both vaguely annoying.

"I have things to do here if you would both leave me to it," she said curtly.

"How about a drink at the bar around the corner, Jack? I'll buy."

"I prefer to buy my own drinks, but sure, let's get out of her hair."

Jackson and Bryce arrived at a small pub, typical of a neighborhood watering hole, complete with dingy windows and worn leather bar stools. There were a few tables scattered around the dimly lit room and Bryce led the way to one in a far corner.

"The bartender yelled over at them, "What'll it be fellas?"

"Two from the tap, whatever's cold," Jackson hollered back.

There were only two other customers in the place and they were both too lost in their own world of troubles to notice the newcomers.

"Let's get one thing straight right away, Powers. Tricia Cooley is off limits to you."

"Sounds to me like you've already put in your bid on the little filly, then."

"We aren't talking horses, Powers. This girl is my responsibility and I'm not sure you understand how seriously I take that obligation."

He didn't say anything at first, just studied the Indian's face. It looked as if it had been carved from one of the granite top mountains he must have roamed as a young kid. His eyes were unwavering under Bryce's scrutiny.

"Look, Jack, I'm a serious photographer and my work has earned me lots of money and fame in the fashion industry. I have an eye for beauty that goes beyond the surface and I see that in Little Bird."

"How do you know her given name?" Jack barked out the question.

"Why, I expect she told me," he answered with a sly grin. "But let's talk business here, shall we?"

The bartender came over, putting the frothy mugs in front of them. Jackson pulled out five dollars and handed it to the burly guy who merely grunted and walked off.

"Thanks, buddy," Bryce said taking a long pull.

"Let's cut to the chase, shall we? I need a new face, a face no one has ever seen before. I need an exotic, mysterious look for this spread called, "The beauty of the West."

Tricia has that face and then some! She's beautiful, but more than that, she's the essence of a mythic romance, what every other woman longs to experience. I can translate that mystery into pictures and capture that fairytale for the world to hold in their hands."

"If your photographs are as good as your hype, they would be impressive! Did Tricia seem interested in doing this for your magazine spread, or hasn't she answered yet?"

"You interrupted that conversation, but you two can talk over my offer and let me know how you feel tomorrow night at the party. By the way, if Miss Angie has a friend she'd like to bring along, the more the merrier!"

He stood up and dropped another five on the table.

"Great talking with you, Jack. I look forward to hosting you at my ranch." He touched his forehead in a mock salute. Exiting the bar, he was quickly absorbed by the passing crowds.

Ranch, around here?

Chapter 20

When he got back from the pub, Jackson asked Tricia what she thought about the possibility of working for Bryce Powers.

"It would be a start for me and I hoped for something where I could earn good money, Jack. Bryce is already established in the fashion industry. I called Angie and she looked him up for me."

One of his first purchases for them both were new cell phones, so they could keep in touch. Jackson found himself worrying about Tricia too often whenever they were apart.

Not a good thing for a Keeper to be this close to his charge, he warned himself yet again. He knew he should have never let himself become romantically involved with her, but his attraction was like a force of nature.

He thought back to his orders from Shadow Stalker, to protect her from those that hunted her and would claim her for themselves *body and soul.* He had muddied the waters with his deep feelings and sexual attraction to the beautiful young woman sitting beside him now.

"Jack? I was saying I wanted to try this. Bryce can give me the introductions I would need to get other modeling assignments and then, who knows. I might have the makings of a career."

They left the decision hanging in the air between them. He knew it was ultimately hers to make anyway. He also knew Bryce Powers was interested in more than taking photos of the beautiful young woman, but it wasn't his place to plan her life, just to protect it.

They had their first dinner in the small apartment that evening. Tricia seemed lost in thought and Jackson had sensed a distance forming between them. He had put a mental block up to help him maintain his perspective in their relationship. His Keeper discipline had finally emerged and took over for the good of his assignment.

Tricia must have sensed the subtle change, interpreting his interest in her as diminished.

He put his fork down and looked over at her pushing her food around on her plate.

"I think we moved too quickly in becoming intimate, Tricia. From now on, I'll be sleeping on the couch, or at least until I know you are safe from the Hunters."

She looked stunned by his announcement, thinking that he had committed himself to her as she felt she had to him. Later, while she rinsed off the dishes, she scolded herself for being naïve, thinking he had genuine feelings for her. *He's just my Protector…whatever that is supposed to mean* she thought, angry with herself for the sense of loss she was feeling. She went to bed early that night, leaving Jack to sit alone among the gathering shadows in the apartment.

He listened to the pipes bang cantankerously as she showered. The quiet that followed meant she was probably standing naked in front of the mirror, toweling off. That vision of her made him squirm. He jumped off the lumpy couch and grabbing his jacket quietly left the apartment.

Jackson remembered the small bar around the corner and decided a beer might quench some of the fire in his belly. He entered a far different place than earlier in the day. It was now crowded with locals and a few foreign-looking men. In fact, they caught his attention immediately as he moved toward a table near the front window.

There were two of them standing mid-way down the bar. They were leaning casually facing each other. Jackson noticed even though the bar was fairly busy, the other drinkers seemed to unconsciously give these two men a little extra space.

He gave his order to a pretty blond waitress, wearing what looked like a uniform copied from a Marvel Comic Book. He leaned back against the chair and scanned the other drinkers before returning his gaze to the two men.

They both had dark, almost swarthy complexions, dark hair worn long to their shoulders. They were dressed like most anyone else in the place, jeans and T shirts.

Jackson was sipping slowly at a frothy mug, studying the pair more closely. Something familiar and unsettling about them began to surface in his memory. They were both very well built, looking more like body-builders than construction workers, or whatever the other blue collar men were, drinking in the bar. They were very clean too, no facial hair and no hint of a five o'clock shadow. Why would two guys that looked like body-slamming thugs, shave before going for a beer? Jackson put his mug down and wiped the moister from his hand down his leg.

One of the men he'd been watching turned fully to face his table and gave him a smile that was anything but friendly.

Jackson gave a slight nod, stood up, and pushed the chair back in place. He tossed a five dollar bill on the table and walked slowly toward the door.

As he stepped into the night, the neon bar sign flashing like a warning signal, he saw the two thugs get up from their stools and follow. *Can't lead them back to the apartment,* he was thinking as he walked faster and crossed the street against the light. He ducked down the first ally he came to, plastering himself against the side of the building, waiting for what he knew was coming for him.

The Hunters had somehow picked up their trail. The smiling face of Bryce Powers came unbidden to his mind and he knew he was somehow involved in more than photography. His uncanny way of showing up after spotting them from his limo and then his surprise offer to Tricia to work as his model, all carried the stink of road kill in August.

His rambling thoughts were interrupted as someone's shoe connected with a discarded can in the alley. He slipped into Keeper mode and breathed in the sour air that saturated the shadows where he waited.

He heard the distinctive low rumble coming from the throat of a beast he had fought too many times already. A beast that had once been a brother, but now was a sworn enemy of the Keepers of The People.

Shape Shifters!

Jackson slowed his racing heartbeat, a normal reflex to the coming battle. He called down his warrior spirit guides and felt the metamorphosis take hold of his body. Still cloaked in deep shadows, he knew his body was transforming into the warrior, Stone Wolf.

He quietly endured the pain of that twisting and thrusting of bone and matter in his human form. He knew this would ultimately mean his strength and agility was magnified to superhuman proportions.

He heard another sound. This time a throaty growl.

Close.

They sensed his presence, and smelled his blood.

They were hungry.

Stone Wolf watched from the concealing darkness of the tall buildings around him. One stalker cast a shadow on the ground nearby, directly in front of him; the other must have gone around, hoping to take him from behind.

A chill ran down his spine as the bones of his straight and muscled back began to bulge and stretch until he heard the material of his jacket tear.

He was ready.

In a blur of movement, the Keeper leapt from the shadows. He sailed over the head of the Hunter.

Now he was behind him and took advantage of his momentary confusion and launched himself at the Hunter's exposed back.

There was a wet sound and a gurgle as the Keeper tore the Hunter's head from his body. The Hunter's torso fell a few feet from his head. Both dissolved into the gritty earth leaving only two stains.

The Keeper completed that task in under a minute, but it was enough time for the second Hunter to take advantage of his distraction.

He threw himself at the Keeper, his claws connecting with fabric and skin and tearing both like tissue paper. The Keeper suppressed a howl of pain, not willing to expose any innocent passerby to the Hunter's killing madness.

The Hunter did what his intended victim had hoped for and leaned in toward the exposed throat of the Keeper, ready to rip it out and finish off his enemy.

The streets of a big city echo an ambient sound, even during the darkest hours. Now, that murmuring buzz was shattered when the Keeper plunged an eight inch curved blade into the exposed belly of the Hunter and ripped upward. Disemboweled, he stood for a second before he realized he was dead.

Falling to the ground, he too melted into the dirt and trash scattered around the alleyway.

The Keeper limped back to the shadows to wait until he returned to his natural form, checking that there was no witness to this attack.

Five minutes later, Jackson Wolf emerged to a thankfully empty street. Holding his arm around his lower chest, he began to make his way back to the apartment. He knew if any cops saw him walking the street at this hour, they'd figure he'd been to the bar and was staggering slightly on his way home. *Typical Indian* he thought bitterly, certain that was the way he would be judged by any white man passing him on the street. Tonight, that was a good cover for the wounds he'd sustained before he dispatched the second Hunter.

He hoped Tricia was asleep. He didn't notice the trail of blood that followed his slow progress until he closed the door on the world one more time.

Chapter 21

They sat at the small kitchen table, moved nearer to the apartment windows so they'd have better light. The toaster they found had two settings it seemed, slightly singed and burned, but they were enjoying a quiet coffee with toast and two soft boiled eggs each.

"I've not done much cooking," Tricia warned him as he ate the over-cooked eggs.

"These are fine, Tricia. I didn't expect we'd be doing more than a bowl of cereal."

She had been asleep when he returned from his encounter with the Hunters, but he sensed she knew. She kept sneaking looks in his direction, studying him for any sign of trouble.

Finally, as they sat sipping their second cups of coffee, Jackson spoke up.

"I went to the bar around the corner last night."

"I noticed you hadn't come to…come home." She looked embarrassed admitting she expected him in her bed when she woke.

"There was a little bit of a dust up with two guys. Guessing they just didn't like Indians."

Her mouth opened with a question, but she didn't ask it. Instead, she rose from her chair and over to him, putting her hand out as if to help him to his feet.

"Jack, no secrets between us," she said when he took her hand and stood. He looked for a moment into the dark pools of her eyes and saw her concern and need.

"I never meant to reject you. I thought only to keep you safe. From me." He was still holding her hand and led her back to the small bedroom.   She had pulled the fluffy comforter over the pillows, creating an inviting nest where the morning sun barely grazed the gritty window pane.

Standing close together, they helped one another undress in the muted light. They made love with a passion neither thought could be replicated until they did it once more. Their passion was a conflagration, burning through their damp bodies and consuming their flesh with mouths and tongues, making skin pliable with hands and fingers.

Lying exhausted against his smooth, muscled chest, her arm wrapped around him, she whispered, "I feel safe with you, Jack," and dozed off, listening to the comforting sound of his heartbeat.

Jackson's arms held her tightly. Occasionally his hands drifted down the curve of her back, as if memorizing her form.

Tricia had seen the merest outline of a wound along Jackson's rib cage, but said nothing, knowing he would share its origin when he was ready. She felt totally at ease with him, knowing in her heart he was more than her protector and lover. He would play a significant part in her destiny.

Tricia had never been superstitious, like many of her Indian friends. They talked about spirits in the mountains and forests, or men that could change their bodies into animals, or even other people. She was an avid reader and those primitive beliefs didn't fit into the world she wanted to live in.

They were dressed and ready to go out for a few items they'd over-looked shopping, when Tricia's new cell phone buzzed.

It was not her new friend, Angie, but Bryce Powers.

"Good morning, Tricia. Just wanted to be sure you and your friends would be attending my little soiree this evening."

"Hi, Bryce." She shot Jackson a quick look, but he seemed preoccupied and didn't hear.

"We planned on being there with Angie and her boyfriend, Teddy, around eight-thirty. I guess you've given Jack directions?"

"Oh, yeah. He knows how to find me. I offered to send my car, but he seemed to want to hunt me down himself," he said laughing.

"You might like to play dress-up, Tricia. It'll be a touch more formal than jeans, but I know you'll be beautiful no matter how you dress."

"See you this evening then," she said quickly, not wanting to respond to his compliment with Jackson a few feet away.

"That Bryce?" he asked when she exited the apartment a minute later to join him in the hallway.

"Yeah. Just checking in to tell us it's kind of dressier than jeans tonight."

"Hm," was his only response.

She slipped her hand into his as they knocked on Angie's door. Teddy answered, wearing a grey sweatshirt and baggy jeans.

"Hey, man," he said, giving Jackson a broad smile.

It's almost like he knows about Jackson and me, Tricia thought and felt a blush on her cheeks.

They stepped into the retro-decorated apartment that Angie and Teddy shared. There were guitars and an electric keyboard along with recording equipment scattered around one corner of the living room. Their apartments were identical, but it was easy for Jackson to see how Tricia had established order in the small rooms, whereas their friend had happy chaos. He decided he preferred the cozy home Tricia had made for them.

He squeezed her hand and when she looked up at him, he reached out and stroked her face gently.

"Hey, you two. None of that mushy stuff, right Angie?" Teddy said, laughing.

"You leave those two alone, Teddy. They can handle life without your directions."

Tricia thought she'd better let them know this was a more formal party.

Teddy was comfortable anywhere, wearing anything he told them, as long as his black beauty was on his arm. This made Angie laugh and smack his arm, but it was clear she was crazy about the stocky white boy. His face lit up like he'd just won the lottery when he looked at her.

They decided to rummage through the thrift stores in the surrounding neighborhoods for cast-off fashion finery. As they were pawing through racks in the second-hand shop, Jackson enjoyed the feeling of being with warm, genuine people.

Two stores and three hours later they were all loaded down with packages and garment bags. Tricia wouldn't let Jack see what she had picked for that evening. He had chosen clothes carefully, wanting to impress his rival with his own good taste in more than just women. He was looking forward to getting duded-up, as Teddy called it.

"This will be fun, Jack. I love what I found." Tricia was smiling and her eyes reflected her contentment. She glowed with youth and energy he hadn't seen before. *This is going to be good,* Jackson thought. *Good for her, good for us.* He reminded himself where it was they would be going for this special night. With that in mind, he lost some of his peace of mind. He didn't trust Bryce Powers and he still had Hunters waiting for an opportunity to find him off guard.

Can't let that happen, Stone Wolf, he thought grimly.

Chapter 22

When they arrived at the address Bryce had given them, even Teddy was impressed as he pulled into a long, circular drive.

"Wow! Some digs! You folks have some kinda' connected friend? This guy must be loaded!"

They stopped near a sign reading Valet Parking. Teddy reluctantly handed the keys to his Fiat over to a kid that looked too young to drive.

Jackson took Tricia by the elbow and drew her aside from the others just before they were about to ring the bell.

The music was so loud, they could almost feel the throbbing of a deep bass coming from the house. There was raucous laughter, shouts and singing along with the sound of people calling loudly over the music.

Tricia looked up at Jackson and thought for the hundredth time that he looked like a movie star. His dark skin and strong features seemed like something an artist could have created. Wearing cream linen trousers, a black silk shirt, opened enough to flash his muscular chest, he could have stepped out of a US Magazine. He had touched off the ensemble with a heavy silver chain, a beautiful silver wolf dangling to draw attention to his last open button.

He had moved Tricia toward a stone fence that encircled part of the front of the mansion. As they got closer to it, they could smell the sweet odor of burning pot. Bryce might not know there were marijuana users at the party, but Jackson seriously doubted that. In fact, he suspected he provided it.

Tricia was careful not to step on the unbelievably green, manicured lawn in her high heels. She had paid a fortune for them, but Angie insisted they were made for her strapless, apricot-colored dress. When she put it on back in the apartment, Jackson just stood silently looking at her from across the room.

Her hair was freshly washed and worn loose, falling like a midnight shadow across her slim back and softly rounded shoulders. She tried to pull the top up on the dress at first, but realized its gentle folds of material were flattering to her full figure. She ran a finger over the tawny mounds of her breasts and felt an immediate chill run through her.

Now, standing close to Jack she held her small clutch purse to her side, feeling confident in the tight sheath dress, smooth under her fingers.

"What is it, Jack? Changed your mind about going in?" she asked, smiling.

"I just wanted to let you know that I want you to have a great time, Tricia, but if I say it's time to leave, I hope you won't put up a fuss. There's lots about our host I'm not too comfortable with and I need to get the lay of the land here before we dig ourselves in too deep. You OK with that?"

She stood on tip-toe to give him a kiss and his answer.

Jackson had taken Tricia's hand as they wended their way through the over-flow in the foyer, into an enormous living room. A crowd of well-dressed thirty-somethings milled around in cliques, turning momentarily to stare at the beautiful Indian couple before returning to their chatter and high pitched laughter.

They saw their friends over by a stage where a live band played loud and raucous Rock 'N Roll. Each had secured a drink and seemed fine occupying their own little island of sound.

Tricia seemed in awe of all the women in their dazzling clothes, made-up faces and overt sensuality. Jackson realized she had no idea she shone like a diamond among a scattering of sea glass. She seemed unaware that every man had fastened his eyes on her beautiful face and figure, the moment they walked into the crowd.

The silk dress flowed with the movement of her long legs, accentuating her grace and luscious curves. The soft coppery tone of her skin, invited touch as she moved through the room.

"Jack, Tricia, good to see you!" Bryce Powers shouted out over the garbled voices and eardrum-splitting music.

He came up to them and deftly planted a chaste kiss on Tricia's warm cheek, quickly turning his full attention on the big Indian beside her. He shook Jackson's hand, smiling broadly at them both.

"Jack, if you don't mind, I'd like to tell your lady how beautiful she looks tonight."

His eyes seemed to be devouring her and Jackson moved closer.

"She looks beautiful every night. Thanks for the invitation, Bryce. Big crowd."

"These folks out here love to party and show off the latest fades." He laughed, but Jackson saw that it never reached his cold, blue eyes.

After a minute they made their way over to the long bar, each ordering an iced tea with lime. Jackson wanted his wits about him in this foreign territory and at nineteen, Tricia was still under aged. Her twentieth birthday was a month away. He was relieved she didn't try to drink anything. He was worried enough about keeping Powers away from her.

They moved slowly through the crush of exposed flesh and showy muscle toward Angie and Teddy. Rather than stand near the loud band, they had taken up seats at one of the small round tables dotting the room's perimeter.

"Hey, guys! Where you been? Teddy and I have been laughing our asses off at all these white folks trying to dance to James Brown!"

Jackson pulled out Tricia chair and situated himself so he could watch the room.

Now that they were seated he had an opportunity to study the scene.

The dancers looked more like they were in the throes of convulsions or muscle spasms. Other guests were forced to scream over the din, with noise levels that could break glass.

His discomfort level rose when a slow song began to play. The room was thrown into a false hush, loud whispers cutting through air, thick with smoke, perfume and the smell of hot human flesh.

It took on the sound of a disturbed bee hive.

The song was past the opening strains of the famous Joe Cocker song, *You Are Beautiful.* Couples were transformed from spasmodic bodies, to swaying reeds on a lake shore. The lights were magically dimmed, the harsh edges of the room softened into blue shadow.

Out of the haze stepped Bryce, an Adonis in custom-made cowboy boots. He came over to their table just as Teddy and Angie left it to dance.

"Mind if I ask your lady for a dance, Jack?"

"Tricia can always speak for herself, cowboy."

He was watching her face as he spoke, nodding his head slightly.

She rose from her chair and took Bryce's extended hand, giving Jackson a quick look as they melted into the gently swaying bodies.

Jackson knew Bryce couldn't keep away from Tricia. He decided to take advantage of his infatuation with her, to take a look around.

He was in total Keeper mode now as he slipped out of the room, heading for the circular staircase and the second floor. No one seemed to take any notice of him as he climbed the stairs, likely thinking he was looking for a free bathroom, or maybe his gorgeous girlfriend. Making it unnoticed to the end of the dimly lit hallway, he looked for the Master Bedroom. He figured this would be where secrets could be found.

Only the invited would ever make it this far. Jackson noted earlier how Bryce brushed off any advances made by the over-sexed women at the party. *But I bet you wouldn't ignore, Tricia* he thought, his mouth set hard.

There was a subtle light coming from under a double door at the end of the hall. *"Bingo,"* he said softly.

He approached the doors and turned one of the glass knobs. It opened into a massive room with soft, recessed lighting. A huge circular bed and heavy black velvet drapes at what must have been floor to ceiling windows, set the stage for some amorous nights.

He knew he couldn't stay long, but guessed Bryce would have the band play at least one more slow tune so he could continue holding Tricia. That thought made him wince, but this was more important than fighting over who would dance with her. He moved over to a long walnut dresser. He quickly set about opening drawers and feeling toward the bottom of each stack of clothing. Jack was about to give up when he felt a square lump under a neat pile of work-out gear. Slipping his hand under the clothing, he unwrapped a leather covering and discovered dozens of pictures of Tricia and himself, obviously taken on the bus trip. Alarmingly, there were even more taken from their various outings in Chicago while they shopped or just walked around their new neighborhood.

Jackson realized Powers was obsessed with Tricia and was studying him since he was her protector. This was a man of great wealth who had gone to extremes to feed his fixation on a woman he wanted.

"Over my dead body, cowboy."

Jackson's voice was lost in the large bedroom and he exited as smoothly as the silk sheets he left behind.

Chapter 23

Jack sat down at the table where Teddy and Angie were knee to knee holding hands.

"Hey! Where you been, fella? Tricia has been dancing non-stop with Bryce. You'd better cut in before he sweeps her off her feet with that charm he dishes out like ice cream."

Angie made the last comment as she closely watched the pair on the dance floor. Jackson couldn't help but admire the handsome couple they made, swaying and moving like they'd been partnered forever.

"Like watching *Dancing with the Stars*, Teddy said sarcastically.

"Yeah. If you'll excuse me…"

"Guess you won't mind my dancing with the lady I brought, would you, Bryce?" Jackson took Tricia's hand out of Powers' and without waiting for an answer, swept past him.

"Where have you been, Jack? I noticed when you left the table ten minutes ago."

"Let's just say, I did a little reconnaissance, Little Bird. I hope you'll be ready to leave here when I make that suggestion."

He was looking at her with a no argument kind of seriousness on his face. When she nodded her head, he drew her in as close as he could and still move. They fit together like pieces of a beautiful puzzle, each perfectly completing the other. Other dancers unconsciously moved away so they could watch them better.

Jackson was as smooth on his feet as a skater on ice. Tricia was liquid grace, bending her body into every dip and sway of his. Her low cut dress emphasized the rapid beating of her heart as she relived the fluid movements of her lover only hours before.

"Wow! This feels as intimate as peeking into their *bedroom*!" Teddy whispered into his finance's ear.

"I think everyone here is thinking the same thing! Look around us."

The other dancers and guests had withdrawn into a wider circle. The band kept repeating the lush cadence of a song by the Moody Blues, playing its hypnotic bridge over and over. The lead singer was doing the best cover of his life.

Jackson was staring into Tricia's deep eyes and saw reflections of the passion he was feeling. Without notice, he simply stopped dancing and cradling her face in his hands, kissed her mouth gently.

Their mood was broken by the hoots and applause surrounding them.

Bryce Powers stepped out of the shadows where he had watched the dance and the kiss. His handsome face had been transformed into a mask. No emotion could seep through the taught smile.

"Very nice, you two. Had everyone mesmerized from the looks of the open mouths, a bit horny too." As soon as he approached the couple, the mood around them reverted back to the crazed party atmosphere of earlier. It was obvious people were trying to avoid the three of them.

To Angie and Teddy, it felt put-on, as if people had to forget the beauty of love they had just witnessed. "These people are weird, honeypot! I sure hope we can split soon," Angie said close to Teddy's ear.

Bryce stood firm, stopping Jackson from moving toward their table. Tricia stiffened, holding Jackson's hand.

"Are you certain you want to pursue this now, Powers? After all, there are lots of your friends here who likely wouldn't get why you began a fight."

"Oh, I'm not overly concerned with what others think, Jack. But I just can't abide someone spoiling my aim when I have my trophy marked on the scope. But hey, you kids have something else to drink and don't miss out on the buffet. It's quite a spread."

He turned on his boot heel and passing Angie and Teddy, gave them a curt nod and disappeared into the foyer.

"He doesn't seem real happy that his good looks and charm were wasted on the beautiful Indian Princess," Teddy said, smiling as Tricia and Jackson came back to the table.

"One could say he retreated from the field of battle in tatters."

Angie was more pragmatic in her response to the near fight scene.

"I hope he's not up there loading his shotgun!"

Tricia shook her head and laughed. "Come on Angie, let's find a bathroom."

"A place this big has to have at least one every three feet," Angie said, getting up to go with her.

The three downstairs baths were occupied and neither girl wanted to stand around like targets for the ever-circling males. They climbed the long circular staircase to the second floor.

There were several wall sconces, but only a few were on, leaving most of it in deep shadows.

"Bryce probably doesn't want his friends checking out his bedroom too closely for souvenirs," Angie laughed.

They finally switched on the light in a large guest bath.

"You use this one, Angie. I'll check down the hall a ways."

The sounds of her footsteps were absorbed into the deep pile of the carpeting as she moved further down the dark hallway, quietly opening doors.

"This place is huge," she mumbled in some frustration.

She found a full bath at the end of the dark hall. She washed her hands and was reapplying her lip gloss when she heard the door knob rattle as if someone was trying to come in.

"I'll just be a minute," she called out.

But the knob turned again, this time it was a hard twist like the person was trying to force their way in.

"Hey, I'll be out in a minute." Tricia made sure her hair was brushed to its high gloss, rechecked her lips and teeth for smudges.

The door burst open to reveal a mythical creature from her childhood. She stood open-mouthed, trying to realize that she was confronting a Skin Walker, a Shape Shifter, a Demon. And he was here to take her life.

Chapter 24

Jackson had been waiting for the women to return from the bathroom as Teddy went to get their car from the Valet station.

When Angie showed up five minutes later without Tricia, he immediately became concerned, leaving her standing there without explanation.

Teddy returned to the crowded foyer looking around for the others. "Jack went back upstairs. Tricia didn't come down yet and he got worried I guess."

"Hey, you guys see Brysh, anywhere?" A slurred male voice broke into their hushed conversation.

The couple looked at one another for a second and then turned without answering to rush up the winding marble staircase. They heard the scream, but with the music blaring and the boisterous voices of the party-goers, no one else would have. They ran down the empty hallway where Angie saw her friend headed earlier. The light was spilling out onto the thick carpeting in front of the open bathroom door.

Teddy put out his arm to stop Angie from running pell-mell into the room when he saw blood spattered all over the tiled floor and walls. A sunburst pattern crack on the mirror that covered one wall looked as if someone had taken a hammer to it.

Angie stood at Teddy's shoulder, peeking around him at what looked like a slaughter house.

"It's…blood…everywhere," she gasped. "Where is she, Teddy?"

Teddy wanted to get the hell out of there and away from the gore sliding down the mirror and off the walls. Before they could move, the door to a dressing room off the bath opened and Tricia stepped out.

"Oh my God! You're alright!" Angie shouted as she rushed over to her.

"Tricia, what the hell happened here? It looks like the St. Valentine's Day Massacre! So much blood!" Teddy was almost babbling as he took in the complete scene.

"Please guys, we have to get out of here," Tricia answered in a trembling voice.

"I can't explain now, but I'll tell you everything when we're in the car. It has to do with me and Jack."

"But where's Jack, Trish? He came up here looking for you." Angie held Tricia's arm in a tight grip, trying to control her trembling fingers.

Teddy stepped in before she could answer, ushering both women out of the blood-smeared bathroom.

"Let's talk later, Angie. We have to find him so we can blow this crazy party, before things get even weirder, if that's possible."

Teddy led the two girls back down the long hallway.

As they went further, the hall took an unexpected jog into another part of the house.

"How big *is* this place anyway? It sure as hell is creepy. Feels more like a Fun House at a carnival! This Bryce dude sure doesn't spend much on his electric." Teddy's words came out in a whispered hiss. His banter didn't allay any of the fear that had become as palpable as a fourth presence.

They only had the ambient light from the windows to check out a series of rooms. Some lacked any furniture, while others seemed to have been occupied by residents from an insane asylum, with broken chairs and torn up beds and bedding scattered around the room.

As Teddy was opening another, in what seemed like endless doors, they heard a throaty growl coming from down the murky hallway. The three stood rooted in place, expecting a vicious guard dog to come hurtling out of the dark. As they watched, the shadows began to thicken and rise up. Suddenly, they were hurtling toward Teddy.

The thing covered his body when he was thrown to the carpet. Teddy never screamed. Just a huff of air escaped his open mouth from the body slam he'd taken.

The silence was sliced through like a laser when Angie unfroze and found her own voice. Screaming like a feeding Tasmanian devil, she threw herself on whatever had jumped her boyfriend.

Almost instantly, she was thrown back by a powerful arm, landing on her back a few feet away.

Too stunned to scream again, she was crawling back to her feet when something large charged out of the gloom. Teddy's attacker was wrenched off him and tossed several feet in the air. He landed further down the hallway with a muted thump on the thick carpeting.

In a blur of movement, the two shapes came together, snarling, feral creatures. They rolled out of sight through an open doorway.

The women heard the sounds of furniture being broken and the heavy blows of bodies hitting walls.

Teddy was stunned, but now began to moan.

Tricia was in shock, watching the unfolding scene. She forced herself out of her fear induced stupor to help Angie lift Teddy off the floor. He hobbled between them and into the first bedroom they came across.

The females lowered him onto a bed after slamming the door and locking it.

Angie kept saying "No…no…no," like a mantra of denial when she saw dark splotches on the front Teddy's white shirt.

"Help me push this dresser in front of the door, Angie!" Tricia yelled.

They shoved the heavy piece and went back to see to Teddy's injuries.

He was perfectly still. His face was a mask of pain, perspiration making it shine in the pale moonlight filtering through a window.

"Baby, talk to me, please," Angie pleaded.

Teddy opened his eyes and strained to see the two women through the gloom.

"I think I got hurt a little Ang…I don't feel so good, man!" Angie held his hand and told Tricia to put on the light.

"We gotta see if he's been badly hurt by whoever or *whatever* that was."

Tricia switched on the bedroom's overhead globe. It shone down over the bed like a spotlight.

She and Angie both gasped at the man lying there, covered in blood. They saw deep gashes through the rips in his shirt and one along his neck, narrowly missing the carotid artery. Neither of them spoke. Angie ran to the adjacent bathroom for towels and wet cloths. Tricia was ripping open Teddy's shirt. The lacerations were deep, but luckily hadn't gone through to puncture any organs.

The loss of blood was another story. They needed to get him to the hospital.

Tricia ran over to the bedside table and grabbing the phone dialed 911 while Angie tried to staunch the bleeding and clean the wounds.

"There's a lot of cleaning up to do here, baby." She was speaking in a sure, unhurried voice, trying to keep Teddy from panicking at the extent of his injuries.

"They'll be here, Angie. I gave them this address and we should hear the sirens pretty soon. I need to get back downstairs to let Bryce know what's happening up here. I'll wait there for the ambulance. Push the dresser back in place when I leave."

Without waiting for any comments, Tricia pulled the dresser out far enough to slip through and waited a second more, to hear it being pushed back and the lock thrown on the door.

Dear Father, don't let these good people pay for my sin against you.

Her heart pounded as she ran for the stairs and heard the distant hum of the party below. Whatever hunted her was doing battle to the death with the Keeper, but she had all but forgotten them as she tore down the marble staircase.

Chapter 25

Running up to the first person she saw, she asked where their host was. The other woman gave her a look of alarm, backing away after seeing blood spattered on her dress. Her eyes wide, she pointed toward the gardens through the open French doors.

Without another word, Tricia hurried out into the moonlit night.

There were a few couples on the scattered lounge chairs. None looked at her as she hurried down the path, her high heels slowing her down on the gravel. The path led deeper into the fragrant rows of blooms and away from the brighter light pouring out from the house. Off in the distance, Tricia picked up the sound of sirens. She prayed they'd get there quickly, but knew there were few signs marking the roads in the area of mostly farms.

It became very quiet as she moved further down the lane. She decided if he was out there with another woman, he wouldn't appreciate being interrupted without forewarning.

"Bryce! Bryce Powers! You're needed! Bryce, where are you?"

She felt a chill touch her bare skin. Rubbing her arms, she wished she had grabbed a shawl earlier. She called again and again as she went deeper into the labyrinth of garden paths, passing statues and a fountain with waters gushing from the mouth of some kind of forest animal.

He's not out here, she was thinking as she turned to retrace her steps back to the house.

The sirens were now very loud and then ceased altogether. She heard the dull thump of slamming doors on what she knew was the ambulance and increased her pace. Just as approached the main path, she heard the same guttural sound they had heard upstairs. Her mind flashed back onto the scene in the bathroom when she had opened the door.

She couldn't describe the monster that stared her in the eyes, to her friends. Or tell them how, when it lunged for her, it was tackled from behind by her protector, the Keeper, Stone Wolf. She stopped moving and made herself breathe as quietly as possible. She had learned from her father when he took her hunting as a young girl that animals can sense fear.

"It's a stink that pours off your body," he had instructed her. Now, rigid with terror, her only instinct was to run.

There was a rustling in the trees that made the backdrop to the floral abundance of the garden. The woods were allowed to grow in their own wild way, leaving a heavy undergrowth and fallen limbs and branches. The result was harnessed wilderness.

Tricia had good night vision, but now strained to peer into the leafy wall on both sides of the path. The sound of her heartbeat thrummed through her body. A movement was caught by her peripheral vision. As she turned in that direction, she was grabbed from behind. A strong arm encircled her slim waist, while a huge hand covered her mouth and nose, cutting off a scream.

It also effectively cut off her air. Within a minute she was seeing blots of sharp lights dancing before her eyes. The heavy smell of musk filled her nostrils making her head swim with its potency.

She gamely struggled to escape, kicking and trying to rip the hand from her face, but the arm wrapped around her was like a band of iron.

Her attempts at yelling for help were muffled until they were stilled along with her struggle.

She was being dragged roughly over the debris on the forest floor. Whoever had taken her was moving fast through the woods.

He seemed familiar with the path, despite only the moon to guide his steps.

Somewhere in her clouding mind, she knew her abductor had spoken her Indian name in his rough voice. This was one of her tribe. Someone hunting her from the Reservation. *There must be a bounty...*

She was aware of branches scratching her bare arms and legs and a shoe, than the other, being torn off her feet by some ragged outcropping of rocks. Her dress was snagged in several places and the sound of cloth ripping made her feel that much more vulnerable.

Blackness finally claimed her consciousness as they moved deeper into the woods surrounding the rambling estate. He had allowed her only enough air that she wouldn't suffocate. He knew her fear and struggle would do the rest. The hard hand was removed from her mouth and nose as soon as he was certain Tricia was sufficiently unconscious.

Her body had gone limp. She was carefully flung over a muscular shoulder where her head hung down his back. Tricia was vaguely aware of her breast popping free from the top of her strapless dress and the odd feeling of fur brushing the tender skin. Then she passed out again with the blood rushing to her head.

They went on this way for fifteen minutes. The moon marked their passage, casting a shadow of what looked like a towering man with a humped back. The constant bouncing shook Tricia back to a sensory kind of awareness, though she was far from lucid. Her eyes opened, but she couldn't make sense of the ground that kept fading and then coming back into focus.

As she was about to groan, something told her to keep still. A twig broke somewhere close by. Still groggy and in shock, her senses seemed to be fooling her. The man that carried her had to be the same one that attacked Teddy. As she became more aware of herself and her surroundings, she realized she was in mortal danger. This was some kind of beast. It would likely tear her apart when it returned to wherever it made its lair.

Father, please help, me she thought frantically. The face of the old Shaman, Shadow Stalker, flashed inside her head. Then Jackson Wolf's face.

Find me Jack…Find me! Then she passed into blackness.

Chapter 26

Jackson had watched the Hunter leap from the second story bedroom. Their battle, though vicious, had lasted only a few minutes. His adversary had thrown a heavy table at his head and then escaped, shattering the tinted glass of the large window as he jumped to the ground.

Jack quickly returned to his physical form. He went into a sumptuous bathroom, soaked a heavy bath towel and began cleaning up whatever showed. He could heal himself with the aid of his spiritual connection to the Shaman, though it would take a little time. While his clothing was shredded, he bet no one would notice, let alone remember, since most of the guests were either too drunk, or drugged out of their minds.

He was thinking back on the unusual attack on Teddy, pretty much a non-entity to such as them. But when he started visualizing the scene, he realized the Hunter was neutralizing the only male around that might interfere with his getting at Tricia. She was his ultimate goal. The fiend would have snatched her up when she opened that door if he hadn't tackled him first.

But now he was convinced there was more than one Hunter on the prowl. Teddy's attack proved there was another of the Shifters in the house. The one that escaped through the window was not the one that attacked Teddy.

Leaving the darkened rooms he returned to the long hallway to find the three of them gone. He called out to Tricia and then Angie and Teddy. Finally, a door at the farthest end of the hall opened a crack and he saw Angie's head pop out.

"Jack! Over here."

Even before he entered he could smell the heavy, metallic odor that mixed with the stuffy, unmoving air.

"Teddy. Can you hear me?" Jackson saw the fair skin of their friend had turned an ashy white. His eyes opened momentarily, but that seemed too much of an effort and they squinted closed above a grimace of pain.

"Jack, Trish called the ambulance and I can hear it getting closer. They should be here in a minute. Tell me what that was that did this to my man. I think it's something you might want to tell me before the Paramedics roll in here."

Jack knew this sharp woman wasn't going to let this go, but he had no time to come up with an explanation of what they all knew was some kind of non-human creature. "Angie, let this rest until we get Teddy safely out of here. I need to talk with Tricia. Where is she?"

That's when he learned she had left the safety of the room to seek out Bryce Powers. "She figured he needed to know why Paramedics were gonna be bustin' up his party."

Jackson sprang to his feet and told a shocked Angie he had to find Tricia before it was too late.

"Too late for what? What's going on, Jack?"

He ran from the room before she could ask anything else, but he heard her calling after him.

"Jack, what's happening?

He exited the house through the same broken window the first Hunter had earlier. This would have been the direction of his flight. Jack felt he must have intercepted Tricia while she was looking for Bryce.

In total Keeper mode, his senses heightened like a coon dog. He didn't crash through the wooded area, but went as stealthily as a shadow passing over the face of the moon. His heart pounded in his ears as he jumped over fallen logs and scrub. The Shaman had gifted him with enhanced sensory abilities. As a Keeper of The People, it was his right to call upon these heightened senses whenever needed.

Jackson now smelled the soft lavender fragrance that Tricia used so sparingly. Overlaying this was a heavy, musky odor of a highly aroused Hunter. This combination of clues pushed Jackson even harder in his pursuit. If the Hunter got Tricia back to his lair, her rescue would be more of a challenge. It also would put her in greater peril. Jackson never shared with her the extent of the danger she was in. He let her believe it was her killing of the white preacher that triggered the hunt. But it was far more involved. The sexual arousal he sniffed on the air would only be satisfied by an animalistic ravishing of her body. The Hunter needed to have what the preacher couldn't, her total subjection to his sexual dominance.

The ground became uneven and began to rise. Jackson realized he had traveled at least two miles. He saw the rounded outline of hills leaning against the moonlit horizon.

He thought he heard a moan, but credited it to the wind that was picking up. The smell of rain sweetened the air as he ran, his long hair streaming behind him like a knight's pennant going into battle.

He came to a jolting halt when he saw a narrow shaft of light coming from one of the hills. He was several minutes away, but knew he had found his quarry. His nose still picked out the two scents, telling him they had moved more slowly, but were just ahead.

He took a moment to run a torn sleeve across his forehead to dry the sweat. Though the night was considerably cooler, his body was heated like a rock at high noon in the desert.

A sound he couldn't dismiss as natural, pierced the night.

It was high and full of terror.

"Tricia," Jackson spoke into the dark, mute night.

Chapter 27

The Hunter reached the well-hidden cave where he'd made a fire pit and crude bed of several ratty blankets on the hard-packed dirt floor. He lowered the semiconscious girl onto the rough bed and stood looking down on her. She was barefoot, her long legs curving in a seductive pose. One arm was flung across her chest, covering the nakedness where her bodice had shifted to her slim waist. Her black hair fanned out across the tawny skin, spilling onto the dull fabric of the blankets.

He took one bare foot, gently moving her arm to expose her breasts fully. Even in the semi-darkness of the cave he could study their rounded fullness. The Hunter felt himself become stiff with desire. Orders were to bring her back to his pack unharmed, but there was no mention of unused. His muscular body began to twitch in anticipation of taking this beautiful girl, laying supine and helpless below his throbbing erection.

The man lowered himself to his knees. He had returned fully from his wolf creature appearance and would enjoy his captive in his human form. He could do that until she was nearly dead from his constant assaults because her value to the clan would not be diminished.

There was something about this girl that made him crazy with lust. He grabbed one of her soft breasts in his hand and then the other. Her eyes flew open, and her small hands tried without success to remove the painful pull and squeeze.

She probably couldn't see him clearly, but instinctively must have understood he would stop her screaming one way or another. The woman lay silent with her hands wrapped around his. For some unpredictable reason, he let go of her and just knelt there staring into her wide, frightened eyes.

He got back to his feet and backed away as if trying to avoid temptation.

A bitter laugh came from the black recesses of the cave, followed by a deeper sound, more of an animal growl, than a human voice. "You are a pathetic thing, Black Dog!"

From the direction of the voice, another Indian stepped into the hazy light. He was slightly taller and as heavily muscled. He wore only a loincloth, as if he'd just completed a dance around the dead fire pit. His features were perfect, with high cheekbones and full lips under a straight nose. His eyes glinted like shards of obsidian.

Tricia could not begin to read his expressionless face.

"The bitch lies there like a sacrifice on our Blood Stone," he continued as he came closer to the two. Yet, you stand above her, with your manhood hard, but your courage gone soft. Watch and learn, my brother."

Tricia moved off the coarse blankets, wildly searching for an exit. Behind her was nothing but dark cave, in front, the hulking Indians.

"Ghost Maker, leave her! She is mine to take!"

With a graceful movement of his arm, the second Hunter launched a knife into the heart of Black Dog. He fell to earth with a loud thud and Tricia watched in frozen terror as his body twitched for a moment and then disappeared.

"My mission here has no further need of that putrid Dog. But I have great need of you."

He crossed the distance between them so quickly his body blurred from her sight. Before she could move, he had pushed her down on her back. He reached under the tattered dress and ripped off her lacy panties. Bringing them up to his nose he gave them a sharp sniff and smiled.

"You are already hot, Little Bird, and ready for me."

Tricia screamed as his forced her legs apart and pushed himself inside her, tearing her with the unnatural size of his member. But Tricia already knew this was no natural man. This was a monster.

He was pounding himself ever deeper, grabbing her breasts in his strong hands. He pulled out of her as she lay sobbing, taking a breast into his mouth. He suddenly pushed the fullness of his erection into her again, thrusting over and over while tightening his grip on her sleek and bruising flesh. His muscles stiffened and he jerked as if riding a wild stallion until he fell across Tricia's battered and bleeding body.

He lay there, heavy upon her, his sweat covering her in the sheen of his orgasm.

Tricia could not shift under his weight and took only shallow breaths, hoping he would roll off her, content with his violent assault. Instead, he pushed himself upright to stare down on her. He traced the red marks he left on the smooth, unblemished skin. They seemed to enflame him with renewed desire. She felt him grow hard again against her thigh.

The rapist knew the Keeper had a deep attachment to the girl. He could smell him on her skin. That incensed him, making him shove into her even harder until her screams turned into sobs. Her scent was now mixed with his own and inflamed his passion to have her again.

"Please, I beg you! I can't, I can't…"

His mouth swallowed her last words as he slammed himself deeper into her wet and tortured body. She couldn't scream. His tongue filled her mouth, probing and gaging her.

He was panting above her when she began to pass out. He finished thrusting and let out an inhuman howl, acknowledging his sexual conquest.

The beast rolled off the unconscious girl and stood, using his loin cloth to clean off. His back was to the opening of the cave as he sauntered over to a bucket in a shadowy alcove. He was relieving himself when Stone Wolf rammed his face into the dirt wall and wrenched his arm out of its socket.

Ghost Maker howled again, only this time in excruciating pain.

He had no time to turn and face his attacker before he was dragged by the long braid that hung down his back. Through a haze of agony, he realized they were now under the dome of stars. Reaching back, his hand connected with the Keeper's. It was enough to break his grip, allowing Ghost Maker to vault to his bare feet. He faced Jackson from several feet away.

"So, Stone Wolf, you have discovered my lair. But too late for your beautiful ward. Little Bird sang for me many times as I used her."

Jackson knew he was being baited, but he also knew it was all too true. Tricia had been raped and abused by the Hunter. When he entered the cave, he detected the scents of two Hunters. He called over to the large Indian.

"Where is your brother? Did he run away?"

He saw the Hunter repairing his arm with a grunt as he shoved it back into place.

"I saved you the trouble of dealing with him. He was weak it seems. He had seen what your woman did to the Preacher back on the Res. He was only allowed to eat a few minutes off the body, just enough to instill desire for the girl. I, however, ate an Alpha's share and the lust runs deep into my being for Little Bird. When I am finished with you, I shall have at her again!"

This time Jackson did react, but not by charging the sneering face across from him.

His body began to twist, limbs lengthened and bulged with muscle no steroid could build. What was left of his shredded shirt, ripped apart at the seams as his chest expanded with rock-hard sinew. The handsome contours of his face took on the narrow profile of the wolf and like his body, became covered in thick black hair.

Jackson was transformed completely into a Keeper of The People. The only humanity remaining was the mission that had been impressed on the very core of his existence.

He must save Little Bird from the Hunter. The beast intended to bring her back to his clan for the Drinking Blood Ritual. It would be *her* blood they would lap like the dogs they were. After that, she'd belong to their clan, body and soul.

Stone Wolf's night vision was perfect, but not a true advantage because Ghost Maker also had heightened senses. The Keeper did have one improvement over his opponent's animal abilities. He had the Shaman, Shadow Stalker, communicating with him through the mental link shared by all Keepers.

This was a way for the old Medicine man to help guide his grandson, Jackson, if he found himself outnumbered, or injured.

Jackson Stone Wolf was not afraid to face this adversary alone. His hatred of the beast crouching in his own animal form now, was so intense, it nearly blinded him to the other's faint movement.

Jackson shook his shaggy head to keep it clear of all thoughts except the task at hand, killing the beast standing only a few feet from him.

They circled each other like boxers, each studying the other for signs of weakness.

"Stone Wolf, the girl will never be yours again. I intend to bring her into the clan as my mate. She has already been opened wider to receive my manhood." He gave out another eerie howl of pleasure.

Jackson felt a mental nudge. It was his grandfather. The Shaman sent a bolt of energy through his hands that he hurled into the Hunter's mid-section.

This time he howled in pain as the jagged bolt seared the thick hair covering his belly. Jackson noticed the Hunter beating out a fire that ignited in the heavy hair around a huge erection.

He gasped for a second, realizing that thing had been plunged into Tricia like a weapon. Her wounds would be more than mental. He needed to end this so he could get her to a hospital.

The clouds no longer shielded them from the moon's light, showing the two man-beasts crashing into the muscled body of their opponent. Claws raked down backs and teeth tore into fur and flesh. The Hunter was bigger, using his weight to full advantage. As the Keeper struggled, his feet were swept out from under him. He landed on the hard ground, the air pushed from his lungs when the Hunter landed on top.

The Hunter sunk his claws into the vulnerable chest beneath him as the Keeper struggled to breathe.

Suddenly, the Hunter became rigid and stopped moving. His red eyes became wide with surprise as he reached one long arm behind his back. Whatever he was doing gave the Keeper his chance to end the combat by lurching forward and tearing out his enemy's throat. Blood gushed out in an arc, covering the ground like a dark, moving shadow.

The dead body was pushed aside. Jackson lay on his back and began his transformation from Keeper to human form.

His eyes were drawn to a movement a few feet from where the Hunter had fallen, face down. He knew that body would be gone now, reclaimed by the clan's Spirit Taker. He didn't want to acknowledge that he knew someone was standing there in case it was another Hunter.

He slowly turned his head and saw Tricia weaving back and forth on her feet. The look of horror on her face was clear in the moonlight. There was no doubt she had seen him in his Keeper form.

He studied her for a moment before seeing the knife in her right hand. It was still dripping with the Hunter's blood. She appeared to be sleep walking as she continued to stare at the spot the Hunter had collapsed in death, a death she caused.

Jackson got to his feet, his left arm wrapped around his mid-section where claws had ripped back his skin, exposing muscle. He had already begun to heal, but he wanted to hide the places that remained torn.

Without speaking, he took Tricia into his arms and lifted her off the ground. Her head lolled onto his shoulder and a soft moan escaped her lips. The knife slipped from her fingers, making a metallic, lonely sound in the night.

Using a renewed power to his muscles, he ran like a dark wind, back to Bryce Powers' house and the ambulance he hoped was still there.

Chapter 28

The ambulance finally arrived at Bryce Powers' ranch, after getting lost several times along the way. They were part of a private ambulance company, servicing most of that rural area for transport to the nearest medical care facilities.

Tucked in among some hills in a remote part of a heavily wooded area, Bryce Power's ranch was like searching for a slug in the tomato patch the ambulance driver had declared in frustration.

"Where's the patient?" the paramedic shouted to the glassy-eyed revelers crowding at the double front doors. Angie quickly guided the Paramedics to Teddy's bloodied body.

Teddy was in a delirium from loss of blood and beginning to go into shock. They hooked him up with an IV and fluids and administered quick first aid, staunching the seepage of blood from his chest wounds.

"What the hell did this, man?" one Medic asked of no one in particular.

"It was some kind of wild animal, likely a wolf." Bryce Powers said stepping past Angie and closer to the bed.

"Wolves? Around here? That's nuts!" said the Paramedic as they carefully moved Teddy onto the stretcher rom the blood-drenched bedding.

"They were part of an exotic animal collection of one of my eccentric neighbors. He warned me they escaped last year from their enclosure, because he knew I had horses. Never did find them," Bryce explained.

Angie knew he was lying, but kept her mouth shut. All she wanted was to get Teddy and herself out of the mad house.

They loaded their patient and Angie into the ambulance and were flying back down the curved drive. Angie could see Bryce standing in front of the crowd of guests, watching the ambulance drive away.

He looks like this happens every day around here. Give me Chicago streets any time.

The closest hospital was at least forty minutes out with sirens wailing. The driver leaned into the steering wheel as he sped up and swerved to miss the ruts and pot holes in the unpaved country roads. Suddenly, he slammed on the brakes as he rounded a narrow curve.

In front of the vehicle was a large man holding what looked like an injured woman in his arms.

"What the hell?" roared the Paramedic as the ambulance came to a bone-jarring stop.

"Look," was all the driver said.

They both jumped down and ran to Jackson's side.

"Help us. She's been badly hurt." Jackson was hardly aware when one of the medics ran back to the ambulance for the other stretcher. He was exhausted from what had been at least a ten mile run over rough country. He had to stay off the main roads because he was certain of one thing, there was one Hunter left.

Angie didn't want to leave Teddy's side, so had moved slightly forward so she could see out the front window.

The medics were blocking her view of someone standing in the road until one of them moved to run back for the second stretcher. It gave her a clear view of Tricia and Jackson.

"Oh, my God," she yelled as the ambulance doors opened and the medic grabbed the transport bed.

"They're our friends!" she shouted at the confused looking man.

"You know them?"

He didn't wait for her answer, but rushed back to their new patient. He thought this call was already weird enough, with all the talk he'd heard back at that fancy house from some of the guests about a wolf monster running on two legs.

Geesh, what a bunch of drugged out creeps he'd thought at the time.

Looking at the bloodied woman and the shredded, blood covered shirt of her rescuer, he wasn't so sure now.

Jackson gave up his burden to the two professionals and let them cover her with blankets. They quickly installed her in the back across from Teddy and Angie and began an IV.

"Get in with your lady, man! We've got to move, now!"

Jackson climbed in and crouched down next to the semi-conscious girl. He looked over at Angie.

"How's he doing, Angie?"

"They said he lost a lot of blood, but he seems quieter now. Tell me what happened, Jack. Is Trish…?"

"She was kidnapped by the one that attacked Teddy. He jumped out the window when we were fighting."

"That was two stories up!"

"Yeah. I found him, but not before he…not before he hurt Tricia."

He had been stroking her hair away from her forehead and was unaware she had come to enough to hear his words.

"Jack," she whispered weakly, her eyes fluttering open. "You found me. I called to you."

"I'm with you, Little Bird. Now and always."

They arrived at the hospital that served the communities in the outskirts of the sprawling metropolis. The medics first unloaded Teddy and then, after the hospital staff took over, quickly returned for Tricia.

Jackson followed as they rolled her through the Emergency entrance and into an examining room.

He didn't want to leave her side, but was taken to another room to be checked out by one of the doctors on call. His serious wounds were all healed over by then, only a few of the minor gashes were left. The Shaman had given his grandson, Jackson Stone Wolf, the gift of healing the killing wounds of the body.

As he waited for word on Tricia, he wished for healing of the wounds of the mind.

She'll need much soothing of her spirit, Grandfather, he thought as he stared at the curtain drawn around his bed.

From the second emergency bay where Tricia lay, fading in and out of consciousness, the nurses had already discovered she had been violently assaulted. They carefully worked together to sooth her while they cleaned the obvious wounds and tearing of a brutal rape.

Tricia was only vaguely aware of being gently handled, getting whiffs of the mild medicinal soaps used on her body.

"Who could do this to this beautiful girl?" one of the nurses remarked, not realizing Tricia was lucid enough to understand.

"He should have his balls removed slowly and stuffed in his mou…"

"Girls. What have we got?" a woman's voice cut through the whispered conversation.

"It's a brutal rape, Dr. Marita," one of the nurses answered.

"Just finished cleaning her up after doing the Rape Kit."

"Then give her a moment for some peace for the love of the Virgin! She's been through enough man-handling for now. Let's start stitching the tears and give her something for pain besides your sympathy."

Tricia faded off to wherever a battered mind goes for respite. Her last clear thought was of Jackson.

Chapter 29

The doctor told him the rape had been reported to the police. A female officer would interview his girlfriend as soon as she was up to it. Right now, she was resting comfortably after a mild sedative was administered.

"Whoever attacked her was a barbaric animal."

Jackson thought to himself how apt a description that was of the dead Hunter.

He let his mind wander back to the scene of the battle for his life and how Tricia had managed, in her condition, to retrieve a knife from somewhere in the cave. He knew she had to dig deep inside herself to find the strength to do what she did. He'd never forget her sacrifice to save him.

He had been drifting like a log in swampy water, just a little distance of peace until he slammed into a memory that brought him back out of the healing dark. His chair was close to Tricia's bedside. He saw her fingers twitch, probably sensing the IV they hooked up through the vein on top of her hand. She moaned softly and turned her head slowly from side to side, restless in her drug-induced sleep.

Jackson stood to stretch himself.

The ER was still active, but the bustle had become white noise to him. His heightened senses were listening to a voice he recognized coming from the nurse's station toward the front of the long hallway. A minute later, Bryce Powers poked his sandy-blond head through the oval loop of the curtain surrounding Tricia's bed.

"Jack, I came as soon as I could. How is she?"

Powers looked genuinely distraught. His sharp features seemed blunted, as if he were wearing a tight mask to control his visible emotions. Jackson knew he was seeing another side of Powers the dandy, a side more human and caring. Unfortunately, he saw that caring directed at the woman he loved.

Jackson motioned the other man to step outside the curtained room and followed a few feet behind. "Let's grab a coffee and we'll talk."

They found a beverage machine and sat at one of the few tables in the waiting room.

"What happened to her, Jack? I've been told so many wild stories by the other guests…some crazy shit about monsters and wolf-men!"

Jackson had been staring into the oily swirl on top of the coffee. He turned and looked directly into Power's startling blue eyes.

"Let's just say, you had an uninvited guest." Jackson drew a weary breath, not wanting to hear his own words. "He attacked my friends and when I tried to stop him, he jumped out the window and later kidnapped Tricia. He violently assaulted her and she was badly injured."

"Sweet Mother! I had no idea it was so bad. Do you think you could give the cops a description of this lunatic? Have they already interviewed you?"

Jackson put the cup down and looked intently at Powers. "I can't describe a creature from my nightmares and not sound like a lunatic myself. I will tell you, he's no longer a threat to anyone."

Powers slightly nodded his head in approval. "Jack, I want to offer my house in the Florida Keys to you and Tricia and your friends, so she can recuperate in complete privacy. The place is staffed by only two people, the housekeeper and the grounds man. They've been with me since I was a kid and are good people. You can use my private jet and there'll be a Jeep waiting for your use at the airport."

Jackson started to object, but Powers interrupted his refusal. "Jack. Please. Let me do this for you folks. This horrible thing happened at my home and I feel responsible for what happened to people I'd like to think of as new friends. You know Tricia could use the time away to heal both in body and mind. If you take her to my place, she'll have the ocean and as much solitude as she needs and wants."

Jackson had been watching Powers for any signs of insincerity, but saw only genuine concern. He knew this was just what his love needed to help her recover.

"How soon can we leave?"

Chapter 30

Tricia was sitting on a beach blanket, gazing out on the blue-green waves of Key West. She knew it was a spot made famous by the past residency of the great writer, Ernest Hemingway, a fact that would have thrilled her before the crisis that brought her there.

She was just back from an early morning swim, water beading up on her smooth, tawny skin, her long black hair clinging to her back and shoulders. Her eyes were closed as she gently rocked back and forth, her arms wrapped around her drawn up knees.

The minor surgery required to mend the violent tearing she endured during her rape, was mended quickly. She was young and strong and her body rebounded rapidly. It was her mind that suffered persistent wounds. She and Jackson had been at Powers' house now for nearly two weeks. She had not objected to the plan Jack proposed. In fact, she was subdued in her response to the trip and everything else right now.

The four friends left two days after Teddy and Tricia were released from the hospital. The house turned out to be more of an estate with at least five acres of well-tended grounds and a beautiful beachfront right off a terraced patio. Teddy had made a comment about the Hanging Gardens of Babylon when the four of them stood among the colorful flowers and streaming ivies covering the walls of the split-level architecture.

Tricia and Jackson occupied one wing of the house, with Teddy and Angie sharing the other. A commercial-size kitchen and dining room made up the common meeting area, along with access to the patio and beach through French doors.

Alone on the beach, Tricia felt herself drifting back to the dark, wolf-like den. It seemed to happen whenever she found herself alone too long. This morning, she was drowsy from the hard swim and the deeply warming rays of sun stroking her body.

Her head rested on her arms as she was pulled back into the darkness of the cave with its single torch. She could smell the overwhelming scent of male musk as it enveloped her completely. Her breathing became labored as she sank deeper and deeper into the scene. She felt a hard, insistent prodding of the delicate tissue and heard a terrible scream as she was penetrated again and again.

"Tricia. Wake up, love. You're safe."

Jackson had seen her from the patio and hurried over when he realized she was reliving the nightmare once again. He knew it was past time for an intervention. Only his grandfather, Shadow Stalker, could rid her of the memories of what she endured at the hands of the dead Hunter. Even Jackson's lightest touch made Tricia tremble with unspoken fear of that intimacy they both had treasured.

Now awake and aware, Tricia fell into his gentle embrace and sobbed quietly against his chest.

"Tricia, we need to make a Message Totem so we can call upon my grandfather, Shadow Stalker. He will take these memories from you and release you from their dark power."

"Can he really do that? I keep seeing and feeling everything, Jack! It's as if I'm back in that awful place with that creature. I can SMELL him!" She was almost hysterical, pulling away from Jackson's arms and digging her fingers into her shoulders, holding back the terror before it overcame her.

"Tonight, we make the Totem and call to the Shaman. I need to leave you long enough to make the circle. We'll do this on the beach at midnight." He had spoken slowly as if to a child, wanting to be sure Tricia heard the plan and could take some comfort in it.

She got to her feet and nodded. "I'm going back inside and try to sleep for a bit. Those pills from the ER doctor do seem to help me shut my head down."

Jackson took her into his arms and leaned close to her ear.

"I love you, Little Bird, and will always be here for you."

It was really the first time he had made such a clear declaration of his feelings to her and Tricia felt a pang of sadness. She believed she had lost forever the unblemished beauty he saw in her spirit. Her body had been violated, but it was her spirit that felt broken. Without responding to Jackson's declaration of his deep feeling for her, she smiled weakly and turned to walk back to the house.

Jackson watched her closely. He knew she was not ready for his passion, but he couldn't help but desire what they had shared before that monster had violated her. He had been careful not to do more than give her gentle kisses and tender hugs, deeply regretting that he hadn't arrived soon enough to spare her the torment she still lived on a daily basis.

"I can't, Jack. I just can't," she had said when his kiss had deepened, fueled by his desperate love for her.

He would be patient. Forever if need be. As long as she was healing, that was his priority and his passions could wait.

He sat back down on the sandy blanket, refocusing on the waves licking the shore with long, salty green tongues. The sun was heating up as it gradually moved toward its zenith. He felt drops of sweat slide down his back and under his arms.

Jackson leaned back of his elbows, his face creased with a deep frown. *I need Shadow Stalker. I can't do this alone.* While they had a mental connection, this Totem was a call for immediate help, not just to tap into extra powers in a fight. At some point, it would bring his grandfather face to face with Tricia, something Jackson wouldn't reveal to her.

He got up, gathering and shaking the blanket. After stowing it back on the patio he returned to their room. What he had to make for the Totem was a Circle of Blood. His blood. He needed his blessed knife to provide that. Using any other blade meant he could bleed out. He tip-toed past their bed, noting how deeply Tricia seemed to be sleeping. He was relieved the pills she took were working.

Going into the large walk-in closet where his few changes of clothes hung, he poked around in his jeans pocket until he unearthed the knife. Its elk horn handle felt rough and familiar in his hand. The light from the closet picked out the cream and brown tones in the beautifully carved hilt. The sides were decorated with a perfect image of a gray wolf.

His grandfather had blessed the knife when he presented it to Stone Wolf on his naming day. *Thank you grandfather for this gift. Tonight, I shall use it to call you to walk among us.*

Chapter 31

Jackson had his back to the ocean, its muffled power echoing around him in a never-ending rhythm of surge and retreat. The air tasted of salt and cooled him as it passed over his naked torso.

He had just finished digging a circle a foot deep, being careful to pace off about six feet across. Luckily, he found a garden shovel in a small shed near the house.

When he went in search of the needed tool, he realized, that the gardener and housekeeper were as elusive as ghosts around the place. They had both made a single appearance at their arrival, to welcome them and point out certain features about the sprawling house.

After that, the shy Hispanic gardener and frumpy fifty-something housekeeper, seemed to accomplish their chores in the dead of night, like a pair of elves. Teddy and Angie were late sleepers, but both Jackson and Tricia were up with the sun. No one had laid eyes on the mysterious twosome since their arrival.

Tracing the circular trench with rocks collected earlier, Jackson's mind picked up a thread of thought nudging him for attention. It was something about their host, Bryce Powers.

He understood the use of his jet and the fully-stocked house on the ocean was not even a smudge on Powers' balance sheet. He knew money was not a consideration to someone with Bryce's seemingly immense wealth.

For himself, Jackson was careful not to get too close to the temptation of money's honeyed allure. But could he protect Tricia from that same attraction, especially with the handsome cowboy thrown into the package?

He had chosen his spot carefully for this ceremony. Not close enough to the ocean to be wiped out at high tide, and not in sight of anyone watching from the house. With no neighbors, he was free to use a large swath of sand leading into the tall, sharp grasses and scattered vegetation.

Centered inside the deep channel, Jackson had begun to form the Message Totem. He had been using his blessed knife to cut the bundles of grasses he would need for his effigy. These he had tied off with strands of his own hair, black and strong as any twine.

He knelt in the warm sand, feeling the dampness through his jeans. Using his hands, he scooped the sand around him into a growing mound. Small amounts of water dampened the pile further, turning it into a malleable clay under his fingers.

As he worked to form a primitive human figure, the sun felt as if it was branding his back with spirit fire. His muscles bunched and stretched, then bunched again as he moved within his restricted zone. His skin glistened with the sweat of his careful work, small droplets mixing with the sand under his fingers. It took the better part of the morning to complete his work. The last element could not be put into play until midnight, the bloodletting of the Keeper.

Jackson sat back on his heels appraising his totem of Shadow Stalker. Satisfied with his work, he stepped over the rocks and onto the smooth beach.

He walked toward the water's edge, peeling off his jeans as he moved. Dropping them onto the water damped sand, he ran into the curling waves like a golden retriever he had as a boy on the Res. That thought made him smile to himself as he lunged into the dark green water, diving under an incoming wave.

The water was invigorating and isolating at the same time. While he swam like an eel, using his powerful arms and legs to propel himself, he began to feel cut off from any other humans.

He reached out to his grandfather and felt a mental nudge in return. It was enough to reassure himself he was still very much part of The People.

Returning to the isolated part of the beach, Jackson stood for a minute allowing the sun to suck the moisture off his naked body.

"It's dangerous to let it all hang out there, Jack."

Jackson spun around, his back now to the ocean.

"Bryce, thought you'd be back in Chicago. Sorry about the skinny dipping."

He had moved to where he'd dropped his jeans and was slipping them over his wet legs, never taking his eyes off Powers.

"Have you been up to the house already? When I left earlier, they were all still in bed."

He was trying to sound and act as casual as possible. For some reason the appearance of their host felt wrong. Why had he come, when he offered them total privacy? More importantly, why was he there just as Jackson planned his ceremony with the Messenger Totem for that very night?

"I didn't see anybody around, so went through the patio doors and noticed someone out in the water. Didn't want to disturb the rest of them."

"Right. Well, I am surprised to see you, but then you like to keep people on their toes I suspect."

Powers chuckled saying, "I think you're one of those rare fellas that's always ready for anything, Jack. How about a cup of coffee for a weary traveler? I had my pilot drop me at that little airstrip near here where you folks came in. I could use some refueling!"

They walked toward the house, Jackson giving him sidelong glances, studying their unexpected visitor.

When they entered through the patio doors, they were greeted by the domestic scene of Teddy and Angie sitting at the long, dark oak island, sipping coffee and unfolding the newspaper.

"Oh my god! Where did you come from, Bryce?" Angie looked from him to Jackson, her dark eyes reflecting some unspoken alarm.

Teddy got off his stool, extending his hand to their charming host.

"Bryce stopped by earlier, Ange, but you guys were still in bed." Jackson answered, grabbing two mugs down from a cabinet.

"I'm not staying, Angie. Just wanted to check in on both the patients to be sure they were comfortable and you had everything you needed. I'm actually on a business trip, so I was in the neighborhood."

Bryce had his best smile on, lighting up the place. Jackson took a dimmer view of things, watching Powers charming the pants off Angie. Even Teddy looked pleased with his special attention.

Bryce had ambled over to the coffee pot as soon as Jackson had pulled out the mugs and filled their cups.

Now, looking amiably over at him, he asked "Jack, you mind if I poke my head in on Tricia?"

"She's asleep, Bryce, but I'll tell her you …"

"Hey, why not stay to eat an early dinner with us?" Angie interrupted Jackson's lame sounding excuse.

"Why, thanks, Miss Angie. That sounds great. Could use some R & R myself. Just need to step outside for better reception to call my pilot and tell him we won't be taking off till after dark."

He moved toward the French doors with the grace of a dancer and Jackson couldn't resist thinking Bryce Powers loved to be on stage, despite which side of the camera he used to make a living.

Chapter 32

Tricia slept until nearly two that afternoon. Jackson was getting worried about her. He knew depression was often the reason for escaping into deep sleep. After what she experienced, he could hardly blame her for closing off from the world.

He was relieved earlier, when Powers said he had some errands to do and would return around lunch time. They were sitting around the dining table, eating crackers and cheese when there was some noise from another part of the house.

Bryce hadn't asked to check in on Tricia again, but when she suddenly appeared, it was like an electric shock had gone through the room.

Everyone was looking at her, then back at Powers. He and Tricia were locked in the kind of eye contact Jackson could only remember seeing between a rattler and a prairie dog. He suspected Powers of having the fangs.

Tricia stirred herself first and moving over to Jack, slid her arm around his waist.

He was bare chested, reminding her again of a deity from Sioux mythology. He had braided his long black hair into a single tail trailing down his broad back. When he leaned over to kiss her cheek, Tricia surprised him by meeting his mouth with hers.

The room was silent as the others stood watching the tender act of affection. Powers broke the spell, clearing his throat and scuffing his boots on the tiled floor. "Shucks! You two are making me downright horny!"

Tricia smiled up at Jackson. He was holding her close to his side now. "I'm happy to see you too, Bryce," Tricia said with a small laugh. "Thanks so much for this wonderful place. We all really appreciate your generosity."

Teddy opened a bottle of wine Bryce had placed on the counter when he got back. Angie bustled about to gather up the wine glasses.

"Hey, Bryce." Teddy was pouring while he talked. "We were all wondering when your crew rolls on through here, to clean and cook, man. It's like they're some kinda' secret agents!"

Everyone laughed at that description, thinking about the shy gardener and the dowdy housekeeper.

"Well Teddy, they don't get paid to socialize with my guests. But I do hope they're providing you with a comfortable stay while you're all with us."

Angie laughed and raised her glass to their host. "Bryce, this place is like post-card perfect. The people may be invisible, but they're doing just fine by us!"

They decided to walk down to the pier about a quarter mile from their private beach front. "That will give my mysterious staff time to throw the dinner together." Bryce laughed with them as they filed out the patio doors.

Tricia took Jackson's hand as they trailed behind the others, wanting a little time together. "Are you feeling rested, Little Bird?"

"I feel fine, Jack. You don't need to worry about me so much."

He squeezed her hand saying, "You are always on my mind, Tricia. Guess you're the song I can't get out of my head."

She smiled up at him, letting him stop long enough to take her into his arms. He was kissing her mouth hungrily and pulling her tighter. When he pushed his tongue into her mouth, she stiffened. He could feel the inner battle beginning to rage within her.

He immediately put her at arm's length. "Forgive me Tricia. You aren't ready for my passion." He took her hand again and they walked in silence, shortening the distance between them and the others who were nearly at the pier.

Bryce Powers was smiling to himself when Angie asked him what was funny.

"Oh, sometimes I feel like a wolf needing to give a good long howl to clear my head. Been doing that since I was a kid."

Teddy looked over at him. "Kinda' weird man, but this is your part of the universe, so howl on!"

Powers threw his head back and howled like an Alpha male looking for his mate.

Jackson and Tricia stood a few yards away and stared. She knew she must have a horrified look on her face, while Jackson's look was one of sheer loathing. Tricia tightened her grip on Jackson's hand.

"It's alright, love. He's just playing the fool for our friends," he said through a tight lipped smile. "Think it comes pretty easy to him."

They only stayed at the pier long enough to watch a few sleek sail boats float by like billowing clouds in a blue sky.

Teddy and Angie decided they'd like walking further down the beach and stop at a local beach-front bar for a cold beer. Tricia and Jackson declined to join them as did Bryce.

"If they'll let me," he said while looking between them "I'd like to take Jack and Tricia to my favorite place on the beach. It's not far from here and I haven't been back here in quite a while. Might as well take advantage of this visit."

Tricia looked up at Jackson, expecting him to make some excuse for their turning down the offer. She had no interest in seeing Bryce's favorite beach hide-a-way.

Instead, Jackson agreed it would be fine to keep walking for a bit longer.

The three of them went on without speaking, with only the ocean's constant rumbling and the call of the sea gulls, drowning out an uneasy silence that had been building between them.

The shoreline began to make a gentle curve around an outcropping of large boulders, spotted with debris from the surrounding vegetation and swept in by the tides. As they rounded the mass, keeping to a narrow strip of open sand, Powers stopped.

Jackson and Tricia came up next to him as he smiled and pointed behind himself.

"Welcome to the Grotto."

Chapter 33

The depression was gouged out of immense sand dunes, extending almost to the water's edge, ending at a scattered collection of large boulders. The enormous rock formation had the appearance of being set in place to help create the remarkable cave.

It had been hollowed out over centuries by the winds and rushing waters. The flat, pearly white sand enclosed by the dunes receded deeply into a shadowy interior.

No one spoke, as if they were about to enter a cathedral or holy place. The sun was dipping closer to the ocean's waiting embrace, gently painting the face of the grotto in pink and orange patterns of strangely ethereal light.

Jackson and Tricia had stopped a few feet from Bryce Powers, both taking in the beauty and mystery of the hidden beach and its sand castle like structure. Tricia began to back away after looking more closely at the cave entrance, making Jackson turn toward her at the pull on his hand.

"It's alright, love. We can leave if you want," he said softly.

Bryce must have been looking in their direction to gage their reaction to the grotto's sublime beauty. He immediately noted Tricia's response. Her eyes had gone wider and held a hint of fear, something he always recognized in others.

Jackson interrupted his study of the lovely young woman. "It's a really beautiful place, Bryce, but I think our walk's tired Tricia out."

"I have actually prepared The Grotto for just such a circumstance, Jack. I've had a few amenities installed inside with bottled water and some energy bars among them. We can grab a couple and just sit out here and rest while the sun goes down."

He didn't wait for them to follow, but stepped into the dimness of the cavern. As they watched, a small light showed through the interior's gloom. Some kind of Coleman's Lantern Jackson suspected was turned on.

Do you want to go inside the grotto, Little Bird?"

"No! It's…it's too much like that…place!"

"Here we go." Bryce called as he came toward them. He was holding out water bottles and taking granola bars out of his pocket.

"Let's sit for a minute shall we? I'm sorry I wore you out, Tricia. I should have remembered you still needed to rest."

Tricia watched him closely when she took the offered bar from his hand. His words sounded sincere, but his eyes held a different message. She desperately wanted to know what it was, for her own peace of mind.

She was all too aware that whenever Bryce Powers was near, she had unsettling sensations and thoughts about having his arms wrapped around her and feeling the weight of his body pressing down on hers. She squirmed inwardly under his intense gaze.

They sat on the warm sand facing the ocean, watching the setting sun turn the water into liquid fire. The slanting sun emphasized Jackson's muscular chest and arms as his bare skin glistened like a reddish-gold Sphinx under its last rays.

Tricia's legs were stretched out in a long line of burnished copper from her days in the sun. Her shorts, worn for comfort on the hot beach were almost as revealing as the bikini she had under them. She wore a gauzy blouse, loose and comfortable in the tropical climate.

"This place is pretty much untouched by anyone, but me," Bryce spoke softly as if to himself.

"It's a good place to come and unwind, I'd expect," Jackson remarked as he gave Powers a quick glance.

Bryce Powers seemed lost in thought and didn't respond to Jackson's observation. He did glance over at Tricia just as Jackson looked over at him. The glint of desire was not lost on the big Indian.

They munched on their bars and drank the waters and when the sun was completely extinguished in the restless, dark waters, they stood as if on cue.

Looking up, Tricia saw the quickly forming dome of darkness. A smattering of stars poked through thickening clouds, rushing in to dull a sharp crescent moon.

Jackson watched as Tricia brushed sand from her shorts and he turned to Bryce. "Let's get back, Bryce. The others will be wondering where we got to."

"Sure, Jack. Would you mind if I just put these empties back inside the bin in the grotto? Just take a minute."

Tricia rubbed her bare arms. "It's starting to get chilly without that sun beating down," she commented.

Her eyes began searching the gathering gloom as if looking for the warmth, lost to the darkness now. It was clear to Jackson that she was anxious to return to a familiar place. He didn't blame her. There was something moving on the air currents that almost felt alien when it brushed against his bare chest. It was as if some spirit was trying to get his attention.

Immediately, the old Shaman, Shadow Stalker, sprang to mind. *He must know I mean to reach out to him,* Jackson thought distractedly, anxious to finish his circle and the Message Totem he constructed.

Bryce was back and this time held the Lantern that he'd used to light the grotto.

"I don't know about you folks, but I need a little help to see in the dark. Not too keen on getting wet this time of the day." He looked over at Tricia. She was obviously feeling the chill air, walking close to Jackson, his arm draped around her shoulder.

Powers kept walking while he unbuttoned his shirt with one hand. Without saying a word, he handed it over to Tricia. "Might as well even the playing field, eh, Jack?" His own bare torso was highlighted in the shadows and light cast by the Coleman. His back was broad with the well-developed muscles of a strict trainer. His biceps bunched and relaxed as he shifted the lantern from one hand to the other.

Tricia's silent acceptance of the cotton shirt wasn't lost on Jackson. He watched as intently as Powers as she stopped momentarily to slip her slim arms through the sleeves. She looked down and fastened the long row of snap buttons. When she was done she looked at each man and read pure desire on each of their faces. It seemed by covering her scantily clad body she had aroused them both.

Both men appeared disconcerted by her discovery.

"Let's get going before we have to draw straws on who wears the shirt," Powers said laughing.

Chapter 34

By the time they walked through the open French doors, Teddy and Angie were digging into four or five steaming dishes and two kinds of rice.

"Hey! At long last, the adventurers have returned! And just in the nick of time," Angie said as she scooped more chicken fried rice onto her plate.

"It seems the invisible cook called in a massive amount of Chinese carry-out! We've already eaten two egg rolls, but there are six left! What a feast!"

Teddy just bobbed his head up and down agreeing with Angie's assessment of their dinner, but his mouth was working too hard on the food to add anything.

"Glad you two are happy with the selection," Powers said upon seating himself.

"But where's the wine? I know I saw several bottles in the wine cooler, set there for tonight's meal."

He got up and brushed past Tricia who was on her way to her bedroom to change.

"My cut of shirt looks pretty natural on you, Tricia."

Jackson had slipped back into a T-Shirt he'd left hanging on a kitchen chair. He was washing up at the sink and didn't hear the suggestive comment.

Tricia looked over at him and looking back into Powers' eyes, nodded. Her long hair stirred as she took the borrowed shirt off quickly and handed it over.

"Thanks for the loan. I'll just get changed now if you'll excuse me."

She was moving toward her bedroom as Jackson turned in time to see her hand Powers the shirt. Though he had no proof, he instinctively knew Powers had let Tricia know he wanted her. It was all too obvious back at the grotto where he could barely keep his eyes from roaming over her body, even with Jackson standing right next to her.

He began to feel anxious, like he needed to complete the Circle of Blood immediately to get his grandfather to heal Tricia's vulnerable spirit. Earlier, he had sensed the presence of some sinister force during their visit to the grotto. Though it was unseen and as yet unnamed, he knew Bryce Powers was somehow involved. His attraction to Tricia was so palpable, it seemed to pulsate like the carotid artery. Jackson was certain the cowboy would act on his nearly savage need eventually. The beat of his passion was hammering away behind his eyes.

Twenty minutes passed before Tricia returned to the kitchen. She had obviously showered, her hair still damp in a ponytail.

The others were eating and chatting quietly among themselves. Jackson had just said something to Bryce that made him chuckle as he dipped an egg roll into some sweet and sour sauce.

"You sure do have a suspicious mind, Jack. Why I would take you and Tricia to visit my special hide-away is simple. I like to share the beauty I see with others who'd appreciate it."

This was obviously a conversation between the two men. Angie and Teddy were occupied eating and joking between themselves.

Later, when they were alone in their bedroom, Jack explained how he had asked Powers if he had taken them to the grotto to test Tricia's response.

"Jack, I can't believe you'd ask such a thing! It was obvious he was proud of that place as a little sanctuary for himself. Why were you so rude? You shouldn't have said such a thing and I don't appreciate you bringing me into your jealous outbursts!"

She stormed from the room and went through the darkened kitchen, opening the doors to the patio. It was quite cool by then, the only sounds the rushing to and fro of the restive ocean and the call of some strange night birds. She pulled the long sweater she wore tighter, to stop a shivering that wasn't totally due to the chilled air.

Tricia was angry with Jackson and didn't want to add his own misgivings of Bryce Powers to her own. If not for her attack, she knew she'd still be fighting off the feeling of becoming overwhelmed with unspoken sexual desires by the two men.

She'd climbed onto the long recliner and tucked her bare feet close to her thighs, curled like a copper colored cat, her eyes full of the black night.

Suddenly, she bolted forward, her heart accelerating in response to a musky scent riding the constant breeze. Her eyes were quick to pick out the source of the pungent odor.

Leaning against the wall next to the French doors, he was no more than a paler shadow. Unmoving, she was fixed in his sight like a doe in the cross-hairs.

Momentarily startled by his presence, Powers heard the sharp intake of her breath, watching her moist mouth open with surprise.

It made him respond physically to be downwind of her scent. His mouth watered with a primordial reaction to the ripeness of her flesh; a kind of sweetness and freshness he had never experienced.

"It's rare to find you without your shadow, Tricia. I hope you two haven't had a falling out."

He was moving toward her, his voice reaching her ears like tender strokes of a finger. Her senses seemed to become more heightened the closer he came. He noticed her hands grip the sides of the chair as if it were a small boat on a turbulent sea.

He tasted the air and inhaled her fright and something else, her body's response to his nearness.

She jumped out of the chair as he came within touching distance.

"I think I'll go inside, Bryce. It's too chilly out here on the patio."

She was trying to sound natural, but he heard the frayed sound of fear in her voice.

"Tricia, I hope I'm not making you uncomfortable. I think you've guessed by now that I'm very attracted to you. Have been since I first laid eyes on you on that bus way back when."

He was so close now, the heat from his body was warming her skin as it radiated off of him like a fire.

"I kind of thought the feeling was mutual from some of the signals you've given off to me from time to time."

She watched his full lips draw back into a movie star smile. His teeth were unnaturally white in the near-darkness of the patio.

"I am with Jack, now and always, Bryce. I'm flattered by your attention and appreciate your kindness to me and my friends, but I have no interest in having anything but a friendship with you."

She tried to move past him when his arm shot out and grabbed her by the wrist.

"You have no idea who I am, Little Bird, but I know who you are. You will come to me freely and soon. I'll be waiting, until then."

Chapter 35

When Jackson was certain Tricia was sleeping, he slipped out of bed and into his jeans, not bothering with a shirt or sandals. He made his way out of the house as silently as the breeze that brushed against his bare skin. When he looked up, the night sky seemed alive with rushing clouds, resolute on blocking the watery light from a hoovering half-moon and smattering of stars.

His sense of direction was keen and his eyesight perfect for a nighttime environment. After ten minutes at a good jog, he was stepping into the soon-to-be consecrated circle.

He slipped the knife he intended to use for the Circle of Blood out of the sheath fastened to his thigh. It would have an important part to play in calling to the powerful Shaman. Jackson looked around carefully, making sure the high beach where he stood was completely deserted.

His mouth was moving in a silent prayer as he raised his left wrist and swiftly drew the razor-sharp knife blade across it, making a vertical cut. Before a drop could spill onto the sand near the totem, he knelt down. Holding his wrist over the circle, he carefully painted the narrow trench in his blood. Because he had used the blessed knife, he knew he was in no risk of bleeding out. He needed to complete the circle quickly though, so he could continue the Calling Ritual.

The moon was still veiled with scudding clouds, but Jackson didn't need to see beyond this ring. The blood painting completed, he got to his feet. He called to his grandfather, using the sacred language of the Keepers of The People. His chanting became a hum, weaving itself into the background sounds of the ocean and winds. He knew the moment his grandfather heard his call.

The sky above the totem became restless with a concentration of dark clouds, hovering like a large bird with outstretched wings. Flashes of lightning stabbed the blackness around the apparition.

"You are with me, grandfather."

Jackson had put his knife back into its sheath, but removed it once more. He made a shallow cut on his chest, below his heart, and used a finger to paint this blood at the center of the totem.

"My life is yours, Great Shaman. Hear my plea for your help and healing powers."

Jackson returned to their bed just before dawn. Tricia was still in a deep, but less-restless sleep. He heard her sigh with a contentment that radiated from her soul.

His time spent in the Blood Circle was rewarded beyond his expectations. As he peered down on her, he knew the healing of her spirit had begun.

He also had his suspicions of the mysterious Bryce Powers confirmed. The cowboy was not merely a flamboyant charmer. He thrived in the morass that a fortune could create for him, while he lived a double life. More importantly, he was intricately involved in the group that splintered off the Keepers centuries before.

Bryce Powers was a wolf in designer clothes. Bryce Powers was a Hunter.

Chapter 36

Tricia awoke feeling as if she had slept on a cloud. Her body felt completely rested. Even her eyes had lost the strain she'd been experiencing. More incredibly, the sense of dread that always came over her when she first woke in the morning was gone. Instead of the dark foreboding that haunted her day and night, she felt exhilarated and, more importantly, hopeful.

She lay still, staring up at the ceiling, watching the shadows begin to evaporate like mist, as the sun rose and brushed them aside.

I feel different, she thought. *Like I've been released from a cage and now I'm free.*

She rolled onto her side and seeing Jackson lying there in a peaceful sleep, she smiled, placing a feathery kiss on his shoulder. He didn't stir as she carefully slipped out of bed.

Their clothes were in the massive walk-in closet off the bath. She dressed quickly in shorts and a halter top, grabbing her sneakers as she exited the room. She gave Jackson a last look and closed the door.

The beach was deserted and she was pleased she didn't have to share her time talking with anyone. She wanted to study these new feelings of contentment and peace. Her black moods seemed a bad dream now and she couldn't fathom why she ever held on to them to begin with.

She still had vivid memories of her attack, but somehow, she felt she could put that somewhere deep inside herself and not have to deal with them, or let them shape her life.

She sat on the damp sand, hardened by the receding waters, slipping into her shoes. She hadn't even thought of taking a run until this morning. Now, she smiled again and sprang to her feet with a renewed energy.

Her long legs seemed strong and tireless while she jogged at a steady pace. She breathed the salt air, filling her lungs with its clarity. Watching the passing scenery, it was as if she rode in a vehicle, instead of upon the rhythmic rise and fall of her feet.

A light fog rolled in along with the ocean breeze, covering the ground and clinging to the sparse vegetation she was passing. The sun wasn't strong enough to burn it off quite yet.

The rhythm of her sprinting legs soothed her into an almost trance-like state.

She was pulled back from her daydreaming at the sound of pounding surf. The sea was heavy with rolling waves. These were smashing one after the other, with relentless purpose, upon a cluster of huge rocks and boulders. They jutted out from a huge sand dune, creating a small peninsular penetrating the water.

Suddenly, it dawned on her that she'd run all the way back to the secret grotto, Bryce's hide-away. A chill began to tingle in her scalp, running down her spine. She slowed her jog and eventually stopped altogether, staring at the cave-like depression. Its mouth stretched wide, like a yawn in the early morning. The sun was beginning to climb higher on the way to early dawn, creating odd shadowing around the grotto entrance.

She would have to go up and over the carved-out dune, or pass directly in front of the opening. There was that narrow expanse of sandy beach, but Tricia hesitated.

Her earlier buoyancy seemed to be evaporating like the soft mist that had rolled in with the tide and sultry air. The solitude of the place made her feel like she'd stepped into a hole in the universe. Nothing moved except the constant pull and thrust of the ocean upon the shore. For one terrible moment, she became stranded in a hypnotic interlude where she couldn't move or think.

As she stood transfixed in time she slowly became aware of a presence. It wasn't near enough to see, but close enough to feel. The fact that she had responded to an unseen person, shook her out of her daze. Her feet moved unbidden toward the mouth of the grotto, several yards away. Whomever, or whatever, was nearby, she would discover them inside the sandy hide-away.

She approached with the same stealth as the sun, moving without alerting the environment to her presence. She had not noticed until then, the lack of sea gulls or sandpipers, or any other animal life during her jog. The sole life force was hers; the only other movement was the endless beating of the ocean upon the shore.

Coming to the shadow-filled opening, Tricia kept to the side of one of the large boulders and peered inside.

There was a faint but distinct glow coming from somewhere deep within. They hadn't gone into the grotto when she visited the spot with Jack and Bryce yesterday. She had no idea how deeply it was carved into the sand dune.

As she watched for signs of any movement, a sound drifted out of the dark interior. It was something she had heard before, back on the Reservation. It seemed like an eternity since she even thought about the Res, but now her memories flared like a match stick struck against stone.

The glow from inside faded then came back into focus as if someone, or something had passed in front of it. This happened several times.

Again, her memory was tweaked and the picture of tribal members dancing and singing ancient songs around a fire in a sacred ritual sprang unbidden to her mind.

She stepped away slightly from the rock for a better view. The interruption of the glow went on for another minute, then stopped.

Her heart felt like it had crawled into her throat. The pulse at her neck beat faster. She backed away toward the jutting rock face when she heard her name called.

"Tricia, please don't be shy. Come in and enjoy some of my magic mushrooms."

It was Bryce Powers who called to her. She knew he liked smoking weed, but the sacred mushrooms were strictly forbidden except to the Shaman and others he would allow. And even this was only during solemn ceremonies.

"No thanks, Bryce. I'm just on a jog, but heading back now."

There was a stirring of the air, strong enough it made her blink with the sand it carried. When she opened her eyes, Bryce Powers was standing in front of her.

She unconsciously moved a step away, but he followed and was close enough that she felt his warm breath on her face.

"You don't really have to go, do you, Little Bird? My Ceremony of Visions has only begun."

Tricia knew she hadn't moved her legs, but she suddenly found herself deep inside the grotto in front of a small but constant fire.

The shadows cast by the flames danced like wild men upon the walls and ceiling as she watched, transfixed and too shocked to feel fear. She noticed a thick bedroll on the sandy floor, close to the warmth radiated by the fire.

Her body became lethargic and when Bryce moved her over to the blanket, she sat down without a word of protest.

"My ceremony is very simple, Little Bird. I call out to my gods to liberate my own visions and implant them in others. That way, I influence their choices, just as I have done with you. Without really noticing what he was doing, Tricia felt her halter top slip from around her neck, then off her back. She looked down with her dreamy eyes and saw it puddled at her side and vaguely wondered how that had happened.

Bryce was sitting beside her. She turned her eyes to him. His face had a hand print in a deep red ochre painted onto each cheek. He wore only a simple loin cloth made of some kind of hide. His chest was decorated in jagged lines like rows of teeth in a deep yellow.

He dropped his eyes from hers now, to study her body. She stood up as if pulled by invisible strings and began to undo her shorts, slipping them down her narrow hips. They fell around her feet.

She sat down, totally naked except for her shoes and these Bryce moved to unlace as she watched passively.

When he had them off she laid back on the bedroll and opened herself to the Indian standing over her.

Chapter 37

Jackson had stirred when he sensed Tricia getting up. He knew she was already under the shaman's influence. His lack of sleep made it was easy to slip back into a deep unconsciousness, especially now that he had succeeded in helping his love. He found no rest, however, as he drifted quickly into a dream that left him covered in a sheen of perspiration.

He saw Tricia back at the grotto Bryce had shown them the day before. She was lying on a blanket, a fire reflecting off the nakedness of her smooth copper skin. There was a huge Indian looming over her prone figure, but she didn't scream out in fear. He watched her throw her arms up over her head, looking both vulnerable and desirable.

The muscular Indian had painted his face with two hand prints, one on each cheek. He wore only a traditional leather loin cloth. There were also markings painted on his chest. These were ancient symbols from the time of the great schism, when the Keepers of The People split into Keepers and Hunters.

Jackson knew this was a Hunter, likely their shaman, and he was about to mount Tricia. He felt as if he were suspended over the scene, taking in every movement. His limbs didn't seem to respond to his need to move and wake himself. He felt drugged, and couldn't open his eyes no matter how hard he tried.

He was drawn back into the dream, forced to become a reluctant voyeur. Sweat poured off his body, turning the top sheet into twisted, wet restraints.

The Hunter was very slow in his movements as he knelt in front of Tricia's bare legs. In a single fluid motion he moved them apart and spread them invitingly before his burning eyes. His eyes were glowing a deep golden yellow by then, matching the jagged markings on his chest.

Jackson tore at the sheets beneath him, trying to claw his way into a conscious state.

The Hunter slowly ran his hands down the lush and trembling body of the young woman. Her response was like an eruption of hot lava as she responded to his knowing fingers, stroking her over and over.

Jackson tore at the mental shackles holding him as witness until he reached into himself to find the thread to his grandfather.

There was an immediate answer to his call for help.

A wind blew through the open bedroom window and over his trapped body.

This is the work of the Hunter's Shaman, Dream Slayer. He has fouled your dreams with his Ceremony of Visons. Little Bird is lost to you unless I can lift the darkness from her spirit.

Jackson moaned as the thread was broken.

He sat up, grabbed a handful of twisted sheets and tore them off his legs. He knew it wasn't fully dawn, the time Tricia loved to jog along the beach. Jack grabbed his jeans and headed for the kitchen. As he reached for the door to the patio, he felt the Hunter's vision trying to draw him back.

There was a flash of light behind his eyes. He saw Tricia, but this time she was lying under the Hunter's long body. He could feel the savage lust of the large Indian as he thrust himself deeply into the wet, inviting cleft between her sleek legs.

His hands were filled with the tender flesh of her breasts, while his long hair swept across her face like a whip. Jackson heard her panting and saw her fingernails digging long trenches into the broad back as he humped like a large dog over her.

He heard himself groan as his hand reached for the door knob.

Grandfather, bring me to them and let me destroy his hold on her.

He flung the door wide, heading toward the grotto where he knew he'd find Tricia. He had to get there before the Hunter could mark her as his mate. His knowledge of the splinter pack was fairly extensive. He was familiar with the Hunter's secret ceremonies from his interrogations of pack members he'd captured over the years. Jackson understood what he was up against. This was no mere pack member. This man could plant his visions and press his will upon another.

Jackson felt shame heat his face when he realized he too had felt the fire rush along his nerve endings as the Hunter penetrated Tricia over and over. He had become not only a witness, but a participant. His hands were gripping her flesh as surely as the Hunter gripped and pawed her.

Only a man with strong powers could stir him to such depravity. Jackson felt the enemy use him like a mirror. His face and hunger flashed before his eyes as he pounded the damp sand, running like a stag down the beach.

There was no time to think, only to act. His enemy was a Hunter Shaman, and his lust for Tricia was as powerful as his vision reach.

Chapter 38

Tricia was lost in the euphoric feeling. She felt as if her body floated now, between passion and climax. During a pause, somewhere between both, her mind was able to bring a cohesive thought to the surface of her consciousness.

How long have I been here?

Just as quickly it evaporated like the sweat off her body until he was inside her again.

How many times…?

His mouth was pressing hard against her swollen lips, forcing his tongue into her when she moaned beneath him. Without warning, he rolled off her and leapt to his feet as if the sexual exertion was mere foreplay.

"You are magnificent, Little Bird. I knew you would be when I came into your dreams each night you've been here. I saw you touch yourself as you felt me reach out for you in the darkness."

Tricia lay still, watching her powerful lover as he ran his hand over the hardness that stood out from his narrow hips.

"Do you want more, Little Bird?"

Her mind screamed no, but she was floating free of its tether and nodded her submission.

But he didn't come to her again. Instead he took a bowl from somewhere nearby and dipped a piece of cloth into it. He slowly and methodically washed himself clean of their shared fluids.

When he completed this he emptied the bowl, added fresh water and taking a fresh cloth, approached Tricia. He knelt at her side and gently washed the stiff mound of black hair, drawing his hand in slow, downward strokes. She became more agitated and began to move her hips invitingly.

Just as his eyes turned toward her open mouth, he stopped. His body went rigid. He sprang to his feet. "I leave you for now, Little Bird. I will come for you when I have prepared the final ceremony where I claim you as my mate. You will never lie with another after that. My brand will be burned into your soul as it is upon your body."

Tricia blinked and was suddenly outside of the grotto, her clothes scattered around her like colorful leaves. She shook her head and tried to calm herself enough to dress.

She knew she'd been jogging along the beach. She was certain she had seen someone, but couldn't remember who it was. Looking around, she realized she was standing in front of the grotto Bryce had shown them. Was it Bryce she had seen? Why did she feel so agitated? Her stomach was in a knot and when she touched it, her hand drifted downward.

She found herself tender to the touch, but couldn't understand why. Even slipping on her shorts made her wince with pain. Jack and she had not had any sex since the rape, yet she felt battered and used as if she'd been in a marathon orgy. Not a brutalizing rape like before, but as though she'd had sex over and over with a lover. With Jack. Except she knew it couldn't have been Jack. Her heart was hammering with the implications of her nakedness and especially the soreness.

She was sitting on the warming sand, tying the last shoe lace, but jerked at the sound of her name.

"Tricia!"

Jack was running toward her, a frantic look twisting his handsome features into a dark frown.

He fell on his knees beside her and took her into his arms.

"Jack, I thought I was still dreaming."

He had his hands on her shoulders, his dark eyes studying her face.

"Tricia, you are sitting in front of the grotto where he…where Bryce took us yesterday. Do you remember anything after you started your run this morning?"

"What? No. That is, I was jogging and came to this spot. I thought I saw someone. I think I, but no, I must have imagined that though. But, Jack, something did happen. I must have passed out because I found myself standing here with my clothes on the sand. Do you think I went for a swim and blacked out?"

Her voice had taken on a frantic edge and he took her deeper into his arms.

"You must listen to me, Little Bird. There is danger here for us. But not the kind of danger you can see."

"What are you saying? Is the ghost of the white man from the Res following me?"

"Not the white man's spirit. He will never touch you. You already know I am here to protect you, but the threat is from a powerful shaman."

"A shaman? Shadow Stalker has always been kind to me."

"This shaman is also from the Res, Little Bird, but he is the leader of the Hunters. His followers are the ones I've already fought."

"Was the monster that raped me one of those?" she whispered.

He hesitated to speak of her attacker and make him too real again, but she needed the truth. "Yes, he was," he admitted.

"I'm ready to leave here, Jack."

"Do you mean you want to go back to Chicago?"

She squared her shoulders with a quiet resolution.

"No. Home to the Res. I want to face these Hunters and help to destroy them before they have another chance to hurt you or me, or those people we care about." She grabbed his hands tightly and searched the depth of his eyes. "Jack, something is happening to me that I don't understand, but I think you know and haven't told me. Like this morning, here. My body feels used, as if we'd been making love for hours. And my clothes…" Her words trailed off as she looked up at him pleadingly. "I need you to explain what's happening to me. You know, don't you? I know you're a Keeper and can see things others can't. Tell me what you've seen, Jack. Please. I have to understand so I can defend myself!"

"Tricia, if we return to the Res you have to be ready to explain the attack on you by the preacher and explain how you defended yourself to the Tribal Police. Are you certain you can do that after all you've been through?"

She looked down without answering.

"Let's move away from this spot, love, and find a place to sit. I will tell you what my dreams have revealed. But know this now, the great power of Shadow Stalker has already made you stronger than even I will understand."

Chapter 39

They climbed the high dune that formed the grotto beneath, moving further toward the sparsely wooded area encroaching on its perimeter.

Jackson had to tell Tricia some very scary and serious things. First off, that the man they knew as Bryce Powers was likely the leader of the Hunter pack that had been tracking her from the Res.

When they had walked in silence for several minutes, they turned east again, hiking to a high point over-looking the green-blue waters below.

"Let's sit here, Trish and I'll answer all your questions," he said, taking her hand and leading her to a clear spot of sand. "Please, let me finish explaining everything, Tricia, before you ask questions. OK?"

She nodded agreement and took a deep breath.

"The man we know as Bryce Powers is a Shape Shifter. He's Indian and very likely from the Dakotas."

She began to stand and Jackson pulled her back down gently.

"Please Tricia, I need to tell all of it, for your own protection."

Again, she nodded. Her face had gone pale and her eyes were wide with shock.

"Powers is a Shaman. I believe he is the leader of the pack of Hunters that's been trailing us since you left the Res. He has been a step ahead of me the whole time I've tried to protect you, Little Bird. While I was able to defeat most of his pack members, he has managed to keep you close enough to make his mark on you."

"What mark? What do you mean?"

"Tricia, Shadow Stalker showed me the meaning of my dream this morning. Powers was the person you saw near the grotto, before it all went blank for you. He lured you into the cave and he…"

"No! I would remember that."

This time she was on her feet before he could grab for her and running down the slope of the dune. Jackson was at her side in a moment, scooping her into his strong arms. She sobbed uncontrollably as he carried her down the curved face of the dune until they reached the water. He splashed through the sandy foam, quickly waist deep and let the incoming waves wash across them, buffeting their bodies.

Tricia's sobs eventually became soft shudders and finally, ceased altogether. She clung to him as if he was her life raft.

The water was washing her clean she thought.

Her head was tucked under his chin and he turned back to the shore. When they were back on the beach, he gently lowered the now quiet girl onto her feet. "Little Bird, forgive me for not protecting you against this evil man. I thought it was only my own jealousy of him that made me suspicious and uncomfortable whenever he was around. Now I know. It was my own special intuitions, warning me. I should have listened and been more careful, for your sake."

Tricia looked over at him as they sat close together. She had calmed down, but her face was tight with worry. Jackson had his arm around her shoulders and felt her stiffen as he alluded to her recent sexual encounter with Bryce Powers. He couldn't bring himself to tell her the whole truth, however, that Powers and mesmerized her with magic until she enjoyed and encouraged the sexual acts.

"I know you are always watching over me, trying to keep me safe, Jack, but this may be my own doing and nothing you can fix. Killing that white preacher has stained my life with his blood."

She became silent and withdrawn as they continued to sit, watching the waves rush in to scrub the shore clean. But it was never truly empty of the ocean's debris. There were always signs of old deaths among the pebbles and empty shells and sea gulls to prey on anything that dared to survive the ferocity of the waves.

Chapter 40

When they returned to the beach house they found a note tacked on the patio door.

Gone with Bryce to town for breakfast. Sorry you missed us.

Tricia was glad no one was there as she made her way back to their bathroom where she took a long, hot shower. Her body felt strange under her fingers as she tried to massage some of the tension out of her thighs and upper arms. She sensed a fatigue in her muscles, making her uncomfortable in more ways than physically, since she understood what that implied now.

She shuddered at the thought of being tricked into becoming a willing partner in her own assault. It was a psychological rape and far more brutal than the physical assault alone. Instead of shock and then rage which she had experienced before, now she felt fear, bone-chilling, debilitating fear.

Turning the round lever, she increased the shower's steam and temperature, trying to get warm. As she rinsed the thick lather off her skin, she saw humiliating proof of recent sexual activity. She was sore to the touch, and her breasts bore bite marks. When she stepped out of the shower and began toweling off, she noticed a dark mark on the inside of her right thigh.

Walking over to the full-length mirror on the back of the door, she used her hand to clear the fogged-up surface. She studied the lightly bruised area and saw what looked like a tattoo of a bleeding moon.

"How…?" she said, fingering the strange mark. It wasn't very large, and she might not have noticed if she hadn't been examining the bruise so closely. "What now?" she muttered, hurrying to get dressed so she could find Jackson.

Jackson had used another of the many bathrooms in the rambling house and had dressed in fresh jeans and t-shirt. He had put on his hiking boots too, indicating he would not be staying put for long.

"Tricia, how are you feeling, love, after your shower?" he asked stroking her face gently.

When she told him what she had found he insisted on seeing it for himself. She felt shy about exposing any intimate part of herself even to him after what had happened, but after seeing his concern, she pulled her shorts up.

Jackson didn't speak right away, but reached out and pulled her shorts back down, covering what he knew was a brand. Another's brand on the woman he loved. He grit his teeth and took a deep breath to calm himself. Rather than answering her questioning look, he took her hand and led her outside. They stood in silence on the patio until she turned and looked up at his pensive face.

"OK, Jack. I've been through an awful lot already these past weeks and I think I'm ready to hear what you're thinking about that mark. Just tell me what it is and get it done with."

Jackson said, "Let's walk down to the water, Tricia, and I'll tell you what I know."

After they grabbed the beach blanket he'd stowed away earlier, they made themselves comfortable on the warm sand. There wasn't a cloud in the azure blue sky and the sun was high now, bringing heat and brightness to the day.

Jackson decided the best way to handle her discovery of the brand was to call it what it was, a mark of possession by the Shaman Hunter. If what his dreams revealed about Bryce Powers was to be believed, they were not only close to a killer, but living in his domain.

"I can't believe Bryce would do something so horrible to me," she said in a stunned voice. Her hand drifted down to cover the macabre tattoo.

"Tricia, you need to open your eyes to this situation. You have been drawn to Bryce Powers since the day we met him at that bus station."

She started to object to his comment, but he cut her off. "You don't need to be ashamed, or try to defend yourself, love, I understand what he has done to you. Even without his magic, he uses his looks and charm like stage makeup to cover any imperfections that could be noticed in his character. I underestimated his power and his desire for you. He's taken all of us in, but things are very serious now, Little Bird. Now he's marked you as his intended mate. You must listen to me and let me do what I am here to do, protect you from being taken back to his clan to complete the Drinking of Blood Ritual."

Tricia's face went very pale. "Does he mean to kill me?"

Jackson had wrapped his arms around his knees as they sat on the beach. Now he placed one tightly around her shoulders, drawing her close.

"I need to tell you what I know of this ceremony. We will both be more prepared to keep you from harm," he answered quietly.

"Shadow Stalker is the only one of the Keepers to have seen this ceremony performed, Little Bird. He was watching secretly as a very young boy, when his own sister was claimed by one of the more powerful Hunters. He told me they bled her enough to fill a small cup and did the same to the Hunter who wanted her as his mate. They forced her to drink the blood from the Hunter as he drank hers. Shadow Stalker said there was a circle of ten or more Hunters surrounding the couple, chanting ancient and evil spells. When they finished drinking from the cups, the chant stopped and the Hunters all began to howl, shifting into their man-wolf bodies, including the Hunter who took his sister and then… his own sister."

They sat in silence watching the beauty of the ocean as it swept in and out. It renewed the shore with each wave, leaving small shells and frantic sand shrimp scurrying in its wake, trying to escape the hungry gulls.

They had their backs to the house when Jackson sprang to his feet. Tricia's scrambled to stand, looking in the direction he faced. They watched as two figures materialized out of the shimmering heat less-than a quarter mile off.

Tricia reached for Jackson's arm. Her eyes were nowhere as sharp as his. "Is it him?" she asked, her voice trembling.

"I'm not sure. It looks like it may be two people. Let's go inside the house. There's something I need in the bedroom."

Jackson had hidden the blessed knife he used while making his Message Totem. He knew if Bryce was as powerful as he suspected, he'd detect the presence of such a sacred object on him.

When they got back to the house he retrieved the knife from their bedroom where he'd shoved it inside a vent. Tricia watched nervously as he now slipped it under his shirt. It was short and wider than most hunting knives, but it looked wickedly sharp when the sun glinted off its blade.

They walked back into the kitchen. Jackson began to open the patio door when he said "You need to stay here, Tricia, until I know it's safe."

"No," she said quietly, but forcefully. She walked over to the butcher block on the counter. Choosing a short carving knife, she slipped it out of its slot and joined him at the open door. "Now I'm ready."

Chapter 41

They stood on the patio watching the shapes flicker in the heat waves coming off the hot sand and slowly resolve into human shapes. Tricia recognized the tall, muscular shape of their host, Bryce Powers. Only now, she saw him as the man who somehow twisted her mind and made her his sex slave. The brand on her inner thigh began to tingle as the two got closer.

She didn't recognize the man with him, but like Jackson, she assumed it would be another Hunter.

"I don't know the second one, Tricia, but Bryce has seen us and they're heading over here. Try not to give anything away until I can judge how to play this."

He reached over to her and took her into his arms, holding her close and kissing her neck and cheek.

"Hey, you two! What will my neighbors say?" Bryce called out, laughing as he and his companion cut a diagonal path toward the patio.

As they got closer, Tricia saw his smile was fixed and so were his eyes. He studied her where she stood in the circle of Jackson's arms, leaning into his well-muscled thigh.

Jackson had consciously relaxed his initial response to the pair, not wanting to let on that he was on his guard. He called back to Powers, "Looks like you and your buddy have been up awhile. Tricia and I have been out for a long walk already ourselves."

"We found a note from Teddy and Angie that said they were with you for breakfast somewhere in town. Where are they now?" Tricia called out as calmly as she could manage.

By now both men were only a few feet from the steps to the patio. She believed Bryce Powers was capable of the most loathsome acts. Why would he stop at hurting the other couple?

"We left them back in town. They wanted to poke around in the antique stores and shops. I gave them my car so they could stay a while. I was sauntering over the five mile hike when I ran into Zed here. We go back a ways. Zed, this is Jackson Wolf and his beautiful lady, Tricia Cooley."

Zed didn't extend his hand to Jackson, but gave them each a curt nod of acknowledgement and a quiet grunt.

"My friend is a man of few words," Bryce was saying, trying to cover his rudeness.

"Fine with me," Jackson commented.

"I don't believe in filling the air with worthless conversation just for the sake of politeness." Jackson dropped the hand he had automatically extended to the man, Zed.

Tricia covertly studied the new arrival while Bryce was telling Jackson about plans for a new boat launch he wanted built closer to his house. The newcomer was not very tall. He only came to Bryce's shoulder, but he had the physic of a dedicated weight lifter. He reminded her of a bull dog with his short-cropped, black hair and thick body. His head sprouted out of a veiny stump of neck.

Powers came onto the wide patio, but the newcomer stayed on the sand watching like an obedient guard dog.

"Need my gear to take some shots of the local color for a travel article I'm doing for one of the airlines magazines," Bryce said as he passed close to Tricia and into the house.

Jackson felt her stiffen beside him. He glanced down at her, taking his eyes off Zed for a second. That's all the muscle-bound stranger needed. Zed sprang like a cat onto the patio taking Jackson down as he body-slammed him, tearing him away from Tricia.

Jackson lay sprawled under his attacker's dense weight, the air pushed out of his lungs with the impact. Zed had his hands around his throat, cutting off air, while trying to crush the windpipe beneath his thick fingers.

Tricia was frozen momentarily by the suddenness of the violence. She ran over to where Jackson lay struggling. The knife she had been hiding at her side was flashing now in the sunlight as she raised it over and over and plunged it into Zed's back.

There was no blood, no screams of pain from him. His only response was a few grunts as he worked to kill her lover.

Jackson stopped trying to pry the fingers off his throat and instead reached down to his side where the blessed knife was sheathed. He had almost succeeded when he heard Bryce Powers voice.

"Just knock him out, Zed. No need to kill him. Yet. I'd like that pleasure when he comes for her."

Jackson saw nothing but spots before his eyes now and these congealed into one black hole that swallowed him completely. The last thing he was conscious of was Tricia's sobbing and screams and the dark face of the shaman as he carried her away.

Chapter 42

Angie and Teddy pulled into the long circular drive in front of the beach house. They parked Bryce's car and began unloading several bags from the trunk when the housekeeper opened the door.

"Your friends have gone for a swim and asked that you not wait on them for dinner."

"Wow! That's the first time we've ever heard her talk," Teddy mumbled under his breath."

"OK then," Angie responded, not wanting the older woman to see Teddy's face scrunched up in his imitation of the housekeeper's sour look.

After she went back inside the house, Teddy asked "Do you think that old biddy ever smiles?"

They carried their purchases into their bedroom and decided to strip off and go for their own swim. The heat slackened as it neared sunset, but they knew the water would be refreshing after a long day of poking around touristy boutiques.

When they walked through to the kitchen they saw the dour housekeeper was no longer there, but she'd put something in the oven for later. "Wonder how long Trish and Jack have been gone?" Angie remarked as they went out the French doors.

"Hey! I don't remember that spot being there. It kind of looks like…"

"Blood!" Teddy finished her thought.

"Where the hell are those two, anyway? Don't you think they'd be shriveled up like prunes by now?" she asked Teddy while he was inspecting the dark mark.

"I don't like the look of this, Angie. That old lady never said when they went on their supposed swim and now…this," he said as he scrutinized the red discoloration on the stone patio.

Looking back at the young black woman, he told her what had been on his mind since their host arrived. "I get the feeling there's stuff going down around this place, just like back at Bryce's ranch back in Chicago. In fact, have you noticed how he's always watching Trish, like he'd like to take a bite out of her!"

"Yeah. He does seem to have the hots for her, but geesh, she's beautiful! And what about Jack? You can tell he's trying real hard to keep his cool around Bryce, but he sure doesn't like the boy."

Teddy stood back up, still staring down at the spot. "Let's get dressed again, sugar. I think we need to do some investigating of our own, and I don't care to do that in my Speedo."

Twenty minutes later they were walking down the beach toward the grotto Bryce had described to them during breakfast. As they got closer to the grotto's location the sun was obscured by clouds. They wondered if it was a portent of an on-coming storm, watching the clouds race into thick clusters and hovered like swarms of threatening dark birds.

They came around a gentle curve in the shoreline and several yards ahead was a huge sand dune reaching nearly into the sea. "Just like the man told us, baby," Teddy said as he picked up their pace with their target in sight.

"I don't know about going in there, sweetie. It looks pretty dark and god knows what's curled up in a corner waiting on us," Angie said, holding Teddy back with her hand on his arm.

"Awe, come on, little lady. Bryce made it sound like a tiny Ritz in there. Let's check it out and then I promise we'll start hunting for the lost Indians."

Following her pale-skinned warrior, Angie took a cleansing breath of sea air as they entered the jagged opening to the grotto. The first thing they felt was cold air. After the long hike there, the perspiration on their bodies became prickly with the cool environment of the cave. Angie rubbed her bare arms, grateful she'd chosen jeans over shorts.

Her eyes were adjusting to the gloom as they walked in deeper, approaching a small circle of rocks. She saw an extra thick bed roll spread out close to the dead ashes of what looked to be a recent fire. Having been on many a camping trip with her dad as a youngster in Mississippi, she knew her way around a camp site. This one was freshly used.

She began to ignore the goose bumps running up and down bare skin and started to look for signs of the party place Bryce alluded to with his comments and creepy looks.

Teddy was trying to start his own fire with logs he found nearby. When it began to jump into life, they both sat down close to its warmth on the fluffy bedroll.

The air in the confined space turned toasty in a short time. Teddy threw on more of the pine cones he discovered next to the logs. The sharp smell of pine and something like incense, began to fill the still air.

Suddenly, as if on cue for parts they were destined to play, they were tearing at each other's clothes, clawing at bare skin.

Teddy ripped off Angie's flimsy halter top and grabbed her breasts, squeezing their firm flesh. He quickly slipped the jeans down and off her long, dark legs, quickly ripping off her panties. The sound drove Angie wild with desire.

Without warning, Teddy was plunging himself into her. He wanted to cleave her open so he could get deeper into her body. His hands had tightened around her hips, fingers digging into her smooth skin. He slammed into her, lifting her off the ground and grinding himself into her.

She sobbing with the intensity of the painful pleasure, but then, screamed as her body became overwhelmed by the brutalization.

Something snapped inside Teddy's head. He looked down at his lover, his only love and best friend and saw blood around the dark nipples. He looked at her face closely and saw fear in her eyes and tears rolling down her cheeks.

He quickly pulled out of her and saw his own body was smeared with blood from her most delicate parts. She didn't move or speak, just closed her eyes. After several moments of barely breathing, he moved to her side and cradled her in his arms. She didn't respond with more than soft sobs.

The fire had burnt down to hot embers, but he knew he couldn't move to revive it. Teddy was barely conscious when the Hunter named Zed, who he had yet to meet, returned to the grotto.

Chapter 43

The Hunter had been told by his shaman not to harm the pair lying unconscious and vulnerable at his feet, but he couldn't resist poking the man sharply in the side with his bare foot.

He smiled when the white man groaned. Then he went deeper into the cave to retrieve the limp body of Jackson Wolf.

Wolf had been shoved into the dark recesses of the grotto, battered and then drugged by the Hunter. The shaman had planned for the naked couple to discover Jackson's unconscious body for themselves, but the spell he placed on the fire cones proved even stronger than he'd expected. When they burned, the pair was overcome by an uncontrollable lust, pounding down their love, along with their bodies.

The dark-skinned Indian dropped the dead weight of Jackson's body a few feet from the grotto opening. He was fully clothed and lying now on his back. He'd wake before the couple, already twisting his head from side to side.

The sun was dipping toward the wind-stirred surface of the water, turning its green waves a mottled red and orange. The Hunter sneered down at Jackson and vanished into the gathering twilight.

Jackson was dreaming. He watched as Bryce Powers reverted to his true identity, the Hunter clan's shaman. He was a powerful-looking Indian, with magical body markings all over his naked upper torso and arms. His long black hair was held out of his face with a leather band around his forehead. It hung down and obscured similar markings on his broad back and shoulders.

The shaman grabbed Tricia, forcing her to drop her knife as he laughed at her pathetic struggles against his iron grip around her waist.

He felt his eyes squeeze shut as the hands of the stocky man called Zed tightened around his throat. He gagged in reflex and reached up to his neck. *This isn't real*, he thought as he fought his way to full consciousness.

His eyes flew open.

He was looking up at a setting blood-red sun; its vivid color nudging him to move. The first thing he did was call out. "Tricia! Are you here?"

Jackson was answered by silence, broken only by the sounds of the pounding surf on the seaweed littered boulders. He got to his knees, still rubbing his throat and crawled a few feet into the cave. Once inside the shadowy interior, he saw two figures lying close together on the sandy floor.

Approaching slowly he saw the pale arm of his friend, Teddy, stretched over what had to be Angie's naked body.

He ran over to the pair, making sure they were still alive. Searching the area nearby, he found another blanket to cover them. He saw the blood that was smeared across each of them, especially on Angie's thighs and Teddy's groin area.

There was no way they were just asleep. They were drugged. He went over to the fire pit and knelt, smelling the ashes of the dead fire. "Spelled pine cones," he mumbled between gritted teeth. He knew Indian folk lore reputed these charmed cones as causing aggressive and orgy-like sexual activity. Jackson looked back at the couple and knew they had been drugged into a kind of sexual hysteria. It was lucky Angie was still alive as that state often led to death by violent and continuous intercourse for the woman.

He reached into his pocket and found the blessed knife he was unable to get at earlier. Taking it, he ran it across his arm, drawing a few drops of bright blood. Kneeling beside the two, he marked the forehead of each with the shape of a lightning bolt.

He sat back on his heels and waited. Angie was the first to be startled awake. She sat up and reached down to Teddy, shaking his arm. Teddy's eyes flew open and he yelled her name.

"It's ok, guys. You're both safe now. I found you back here. You were both in a deep sleep."

They looked at Jackson and then back at one another. Their faces showing unspoken fear. They both finally realized their naked state. Angie pulling the blanket over her bare breasts, her eyes downcast.

Teddy was more direct in his response. "What the hell, man? We came here looking for you and instead, you find us like Adam and Eve after they got tossed!"

Jackson shook his head. "Don't worry Teddy. You two were drugged by the cones you tossed into the fire. I need you to get dressed and meet me back at the beach house. I have lots to explain to you."

He left them quickly, hearing their raised voices filter into the thickening night air. There was fear and confusion in their fading conversation. Jackson imagined them scurrying about, searching for clothing. He knew they were anxious to get away from the place where they had turned from lovers into animals in frenzied rut.

He was mentally reaching for the thread to Shadow Stalker. The Blood Ritual was at hand and he needed the great shaman's help. Little Bird was to be the sacrifice, chosen many months ago by the Hunter's own shaman, Dream Slayer. Jackson knew she'd be lost to him forever if she entered the Hunter's Clan as the mate to its evil and powerful shifter.

Bryce had taken Tricia back to the Reservation, of this, Jackson was positive.

That was the only place the Blood Ritual could be held. His grandfather, Shadow Stalker had described it as sadistic and dehumanizing to its victims.

When Jackson told Tricia about the Blood Ritual, he gave her only a glimpse into that evil ceremony. As he ran down the beach toward the house, he recalled it in every gruesome detail.

The young boy, Shadow Stalker, living up to his name, had hidden himself under a pile of animal skins in the shaman's lodge. His sister had been heavily drugged and was unresponsive to his prodding as he tried to wake her. When they came to take her to the circle for the Blood Ritual, he crept out from under the heavy skins and watched through the narrow opening in the tent flap.

She was stripped naked and lay upon a long slate surface. The nearly full moon washed over her body, transforming her light red complexion into a creamy ochre. The shaman was naked. His erection stood out like the prow of a ship as he stood next to the young girl.

A knife suddenly flashed in the moonlight and he began making small cuts over her body. His sister was bleeding copiously from the knife wounds as the circle of Hunters waited for small bowls, set about the altar, to fill. Each Hunter sipped at his portion of her life blood to complete the ceremony in a frenzy of howls and ritual copulation with the victim.

Jackson's grandfather, Shadow Stalker, had never seen his sister again, not in her human form. He told his grandson he believed he saw her on several occasions when the Keepers of The People did battle with the Hunter Clan. He prayed he would never have to take her life.

This vivid story haunted Jackson as he thought of Tricia facing the same ceremony of death, and eternal life as a demon. Would this be her fate? Could he save her from her enslavement by the shaman she knew as Bryce Powers?

If not, she would be his slave, body and soul.

Chapter 44

The three friends were packed and ready to leave. On their walk back from the grotto, Angie summed up the way they were all feeling. "Paradise is overrun with snakes."

Jackson used their walking time to give them an abbreviated version of what was going on. They were both outraged when he told them about the perverted preacher and Tricia. He wasn't sure how they'd cotton to the idea of his being sent by his grandfather to protect Tricia, but they seemed exceptionally open to the idea.

"There's been every kind of mystical cult stuff in my family for centuries, man. Bryce being a Hunter is no stretch for me," she explained. Angie was quick to accept the mystical powers employed by a shaman, because of a family history of dabbling in the occult. Having deep family roots in the Parishes of New Orleans, her family could trace their history back to the slave block that introduced her line to this continent. "Since your grandfather is a shaman, he can maybe help us get Tricia back from this Hunter dude," Angie stated emphatically.

Teddy was fascinated by Jackson's role as a Keeper of The People, especially after he explained how he'd already fought off several other Hunters. By the time they arrived back at the beach house his friends were looking at him with some awe and a touch of fear.

Just as well they fear me a little, he thought as he left them to pack his and Tricia's things. He knew they might have to see him in his Keeper form. He couldn't let that make him hesitate if he needed to fight.

They took all the bags and loaded them into the car they'd been using since they arrived. The plan was to get the couple back to Chicago and safely away from Bryce Powers and his henchmen.

They all wondered about the housekeeper and gardener when Angie suggested they might be more than servants.

The sun had long been replaced by the moon and a sea of stars, scattered like silver coins across the endless night sky, reflecting on the infinite ocean below.

The trio moved in silence, not knowing if they were watched. For some reason, Angie seemed more anxious about the possibility of the stern housekeeper showing up than of the shy grounds keeper. She kept looking around as the men stuffed the bags into the seemingly smaller vehicle.

"This dude should have bought an American car, man. Give me a big ol' Lincoln any da …" Teddy was cut off when they all heard a howl that sounded like a tornado warning. It hung on the sultry night air like a bad odor.

Jackson and Teddy froze. Angie sprang to Teddy's side, clutching his arm, her dark eyes wide with terror. "It's her! The house keeper. She's coming for us," she was nearly babbling with a growing hysteria.

"I want you two to get out of here, now! I know what's coming and it won't be anyone wearing an apron! Teddy, drive like the devil's chasing you, because he will have sent his Hunters to find you. Don't stop for anything, or anyone. Got it?"

Teddy was nodding his head vigorously and opened the door for Angie. "Get in baby. We are so outta here!"

Jackson watched the tail lights until they disappeared and then went back inside the house.

His friends would take the first flight out of the Keys and back to Chicago and that was one less worry for him. He needed a clear head to face what he knew was coming for him like a shark pack on the scent of blood.

Jackson gave a bark of laughter thinking of the irony of how they'd be safer on the big city's streets than in this nearly deserted Paradise. *I can't let them corner me here,* he was thinking as he gathered some weapons to add to his small arsenal. So far that amounted to his blessed knife and a short-handled meat carver.

He reached deeply inside himself to establish the mental connection with his grandfather. Everything in the kitchen disappeared into a searing whiteness, the place he always met with Shadow Stalker.

"I am here, Stone Wolf. Tell me of this evil you face."

"Grandfather, the demon is unleashed. Little Bird will be taken back to the Res to complete the Hunter's Blood Ritual. I have learned this is no ordinary Hunter who took her, but their shaman. He is foul like a cesspit. He can enter the minds of his victims to manipulate them to his will. He uses this power to control them for his own purpose and pleasure."

His grandfather spoke into the whiteness of Stone Wolf's silence. "You will be attacked by two Hunters of this shaman's clan, left to stop you from pursuing this black-hearted coyote. I will join you when you return home to find Little Bird. You must prevail my son, before she is lost to us and you, past your own life span and hundreds more.

For now, I bring the bite of a thousand wolves to your teeth, the sting of a million hornets to your fists, the strength of the Chiye-Tanka, savage god for our people to your arms. You shall overcome these mange-ridden vermin! You are Stone Wolf, Keeper of the People!"

Jackson again stood in the faintly-lit kitchen and knew he was invincible.

"Let them come soon," he said with a tight smile. He felt the familiar sensation of his body as it went through the transformation from magnificent warrior, to deadly Keeper.

His howl would soon bring his enemies.

Chapter 45

The night was still, only the constant thrumming of the restive ocean filling its vast emptiness. A thin fog that had begun to roll in earlier had thickened until it smothered the beach house under its grey body.

The two Hunters smelled the damp air, quickly finding their prey. Their own pungent odor trailed the pair, riding the waves of air current, an invisible specter. They approached a blur of light, straining to pierce the dense mist. Leather loin cloths girdled their hips, and their bodies were painted a pasty white, effectively letting them become part of the fog. They each had tied their long black hair into a single braid, swinging snake-like down their strong backs.

Jackson had switched on the light over the stove, using it as a beacon to draw his enemies in. He knew they would come at him separately, cutting off any retreat if the first attacker failed to subdue him and he tried to escape.

The Hunters split up, the biggest entering the house through the patio doors, and the other using a back door off the garage. They worked their way methodically, going room to room, until the house was scoured for the Keeper's hiding place.

They had been sniffing like dogs for any scent of their quarry, but the house held no clue. It was as if the Keeper had erased his scent from the moist air and supplanted it with the smell of brine and seaweed.

In fact, Shadow Stalker had done just that, throwing them off Stone Wolf's scent.

Jackson waited patiently for their inevitable mistake.

They split again after meeting up on the threshold to the kitchen, the biggest leaving the house to search the grounds. This left a single, vague shape moving once more through the house, a long knife clutched in each hand. Occasionally, a glint from the deadly blades winked in the near darkness when a weak light slid off them.

Jackson had counted on the Hunters staying in their human forms, confident in their superior numbers. Those odds had shifted now, as the lone Hunter entered the kitchen on his way outside to declare the house empty.

As he passed by the commercial-sized refrigerator, Jackson leapt down on him from his crouch atop the stainless behemoth.

The Hunter staggered to his knees with the weight and dropped one of the knives.

Before he could make a sound, Jackson had his own knife deep in his carotid and sliced through the neck as if it was a loaf of bread.

The head rolled onto the tile floor, where Jackson saw it reflected back at him in the high gloss of the stainless steel freezer compartment. Within a minute his body evaporated, becoming a rising steam from the floor.

Now the odds were even.

Jackson made his way outside where he resumed his human form, but not before he used his hyper-sensitive abilities to locate the big Hunter. He found him heading toward the back yard and the kidney-shaped swimming pool.

A layer of heavy fog had settled over the aqua green water, masking its location. Lounge chairs were stacked to one side, their pillows piled up on the long, glass patio table.

Jackson veered off to the right of where he knew the pool lay shrouded in mist. He had an advantage over his adversary. He knew his way around the property. He decided to draw his enemy to him so he could deal with him quickly and begin his own hunt for Tricia.

Picking up one of the heavy lounge chair pillows he deftly tossed it into the masked center of the green-blue water. The ensuing splash sounded like a body had jumped, or mistakenly, fallen in. Jackson was frozen in a crouch, waiting for the Hunter to make his move.

There was a subtle shifting of the mist close to the ladder leading down to the twelve foot end. Jackson knew the Hunter was scanning the mist, just as he had done, searching for any displacement of fog, signifying movement.

Holding his blessed knife in one hand, the meat carver in the other, Jackson moved up behind the ladder. He could smell the rich body musk pouring off his adrenalin-pumped adversary. He silently thanked his grandfather for his heightened senses.

Creeping as silently as the moist fog, Jackson was behind the Hunter now. The big man had stepped down two rungs of the ladder without as much as a ripple splashing the sides of the pool. He was a consummate stalker and Jackson had no doubt a fierce warrior.

Jackson felt, rather than heard, the Hunter begin to climb back onto the cement. With a blood-curdling cry he launched himself, taking the big man down to the bottom.

His surprise attack caused the Hunter to drop one of his weapons, though he still held tightly to a razor sharp fillet knife. He brought this up as rapidly as the heavy water at the bottom allowed him, connecting with Jackson left arm. The cut was not long, but deep, cutting into the flesh of his upper arm.

Lying under the blanket of heavy fog, the pool was as dark as a bottomless well.

The Hunter was a trained killer and shark-like, smelled the blood he had drawn in the inky waters.

Jackson ignored the neat slice to his arm and instead focused his senses on his opponent's next move.

He had lost the small cleaver when he got cut, so brought up the blessed knife in his right hand. Trying to guess how his enemy's body was positioned, he drew it up in at a sharp angle. He was just shy of his target and sliced into the Hunter's thickly muscled thigh, close to the femoral artery.

There was only a momentary halt to the Hunter's attack. Jackson knew he'd missed the key to imminent death for his adversary. He moved quickly, breaking contact with the bigger man, swiftly paddling backward out of his reach. The blood was steadily being washed from his arm. Jackson knew he'd weaken if he couldn't staunch the flow soon. He was able to make-out a dark form in the water, realizing the Hunter was moving too.

The Hunter began to shoot to the surface to fill his lungs and perhaps see how badly he'd been hurt. Jackson quickly followed suit, but at a good distance from his enemy. The fog drifted just above the water line, thick as cotton gauze. Jackson made sure he was close to a side of the pool. Grabbing hold of the edge, he hauled himself out of the water in one smooth upward lunge for the surface.

The dense mist diffused and distorted sounds, buffering his reentry poolside enough to throw off the Hunter's pursuit momentarily. He silently knelt on the cold cement, working to control his breathing until it became steady. He felt warm blood running down his cut arm. The coppery smell would draw the Hunter unless he covered it quickly.

There was a sound nearby. The soft patter of dripping water. The Hunter had gotten out of the pool almost simultaneously with him. Jackson froze where he crouched, listening. He shifted the blessed knife, holding it down low in front of his body.

He decided to move back toward the house. Clearly, fighting the huge Hunter in the pool would give him no advantage.

Jackson knew the layout of the pool area well, avoiding furniture and potted plants, he moved as stealthily as a mountain lion toward the house. He easily found the stone steps leading up to the open patio doors. He climbed them in a crouch, to avoid making too much of a ripple in the heavy curtain of mist. Once inside, he shut off the stove light and hunkered down beside the island.

It was inevitable that the Hunter would follow quickly, but Jackson knew it wouldn't be the Hunter in human form that would be coming for him.

Crouching lower, he rested both his hands on the floor and allowed the current of change to course freely through his body.

This was what Shadow Stalker meant. He would give him the strength of the beast that possessed his body, the body of a Keeper.

His wait was brief. There was a sound that could have been the distant waves hitting the shore, it was so indistinct. The Keeper tilted his shaggy head upward, sniffing the air. He recognized the stringent scent of the Hunter's own transformation.

He saw a dark form enter through the doorway. With only a narrow, ambient light, he made out a hunched figure, broad shoulders slightly back-lit against the pale haze. The arms would be longer and like the rest of the body, they would be covered in coarse, black hair. The Hunter's strength already prodigious, could be almost god-like in this form.

The Keeper now rose from behind the island, his own transformation complete. When the Hunter detected movement in the shadows, he knew his enemy was ready to complete the battle to the death. He launched himself at the Keeper and connected. As he raked the Keeper's back with long claws, the sound of tearing flesh could be heard. He pulled the Keeper into a deadly grip.

The Keeper had planned for this kind of attack and brought the blessed knife up under the right arm of the Hunter, ripping into it until he hit bone and severed tendons. He was able to break the Hunter's hold on him, pushing his arms apart and exposing his neck. He sprang like a fierce cat and tore into the vulnerable throat of his opponent. The arterial spray covered his face in hot, dark blood and coated the thick hair on his body.

The Hunter sank to the floor with a sigh escaping his destroyed larynx. When he was completely still, the Keeper shot a quick tongue from between his tooth-filled jaws and lapped the blood from his muzzle. It was over. His body began to quiver and he sank to his knees.

The body of the Hunter was beginning its journey back to the Spirt Takers and vanished before his yellow eyes.

Jackson went through the change, back to human form, and was left kneeling in the large pool of blood that marked his victory. He stood unsteadily, slowly making his way into the bedroom he had shared with his love.

Soon, he would begin yet another battle.

This fight would be for the very soul of Little Bird. The shaman that held her knew he would never stop until he freed her, or he was dead.

Chapter 46

Tricia ceased her struggles against the arms that encircled her like steel bands. She knew Bryce was too strong and she was only succeeding in exhausting herself. A feeling of inevitability seeped into her consciousness and she slowly became still in his tight grip.

I will be calm. Jack will come . . . Jack will come… She repeated this in her head like a mantra, until she began to relax.

"Good. I am pleased to see you have accepted your fate, Little Bird."

Bryce Powers no longer wore the disguise of a rich, playboy. His reddish blond hair was gone. It now flowed midnight black over his bare chest and brawny shoulders. The piercing blue eyes that studied her were now inky, flat pools.

He had reverted back to his natural form, a powerfully built Native American Indian. He was no less handsome or desirable and Tricia hated herself for admitting to the sexual yearning he aroused in her with his nearness.

"I have accepted nothing, Bryce . . . or whatever you are called."

"I have had many names, over a long span of time, but you shall know me as the shaman of this clan, Dream Slayer."

He had loosened his tight hold, but kept her body close enough to his that she could feel his rising sex throbbing against her flat stomach.

"When you and I have completed our Blood Ritual, you will share my magical powers, along with my bed, for time without end."

Before she could respond, he pressed his mouth down hard against her already bruised lips. His tongue probed and explored her mouth. She felt him take both her wrists into one large hand and held her arms above her head as if she was secured by chains. His free hand began to tease and pull the aroused nipples under her thin blouse.

Without realizing it, she was moaning, her body twisting. She had closed her eyes, but they flew open at the sound of cloth ripping. Her clothes were torn away from her body as he held her suspended. He slammed her against the wall, but not before she saw his engorged member standing at the ready like a battering ram.

"Say my name, Little Bird! Say it!"

He pushed himself deeply into her and let her hang impaled before he moved.

"Say it, if you want to feel the pleasure I can bring you now. Say it!"

His name seemed to come from another voice, someone Tricia didn't recognize. "Dream Slayer, Dream Slayer, Dream Slaaaaa.."

She was sobbing with sexual relief from the passion he had built in her like a firestorm. He was still hard and deeply imbedded in her, letting her dangle a few inches off the floor like a used marionette. He looped his free arm under one of her legs for support.

Tricia was panting while he slowly released her wrists and let her arms drop to her sides. His hand never stopped exploring her while he used his weight pressing against her body to help steady her as she continued to ride him.

She could feel his erection stiffen and enlarge now that she had climaxed. It moved and jerked inside her and she let out a deep groan while her hands found his buttocks. She dug her fingers into him, forcing him to slam into her again and again. He was suddenly lost in his own delirium, gripping her arm and tearing at her mouth, her neck, her breasts.

There was an explosion inside her and then hot liquid streaming down her legs onto the floor. With unlikely gentleness, Dream

Slayer lowered Tricia to the floor where he scooped her into his arms and carried her into a bedroom.

"This is ours, Little Bird. This is where I shall possess you until the oceans are dry and the sun dies above us. My passion cannot be satisfied with merely one lifetime. We shall share many."

He laid her on a huge circular bed. She vaguely realized it was covered in the furs of many wolves. She felt the softness of the fine coats and melted into the deep pile. She drifted off into a dark place where she stood alone on a dirt road back on the Res. She looked around herself and then up at the sky. It was covered with churning storm clouds, moving like giant gray boulders, tossed around in a cataclysmic event. There was no light save the watery reflection of a half-moon, struggling to dominate the wild night.

Suddenly she felt vulnerable and afraid. The sheer emptiness of the place smothered her with its vastness. She was vainly searching some shelter from the coming storm when a yellow light appeared a short distance away.

It moved back and forth, swinging with the rhythm of a pendulum, growing larger and larger. Eventually, the light resolved itself into the kind, old face of Shadow Stalker and Tricia knew she'd be safe.

Chapter 47

Jackson stayed at the beach house long enough to dress and gather up their things. He knew the Hunter's shaman would have used the private jet to return with Tricia to the Res in the guise of Bryce Powers.

Shadow Stalker assured him he had time to prepare for his journey back to South Dakota. "He has powerful and dark magic to work his ways on her, Stone Wolf, but my powers will protect Little Bird's spirit until you come," the old Shaman stated emphatically.

He used the last of his money to hire a private pilot to fly him to the small airstrip Powers likely used, bordering the Res. The pilot had flown as a crop duster and was unemployed. Jackson waved five grand under his nose and after giving the big Indian a quick look-over, he scooped up the cash.

When the small plane landed with its lone passenger, the sun was just rising over the bleak mountains in the distance. Jackson grabbed his bags and threw the man another grand, thanking him with a curt nod as he deplaned.

He needed a car. He made his way over to a tiny shed with a large sign hanging from its roof declaring it, High Mountain Car Rentals. The attendant wore his long, steel gray hair in braids, a beaded band wrapped around his creased forehead. He sat just outside the shed door and appeared to be dozing, his legs stretched out in front of him and his head resting on a ratty flannel shirt.

At the sound of Jackson's boots scrapping on the gravel of the yard, he looked up.

"Stone Wolf! You have returned from the land of the white eyes at last. How was it, man?" he asked, smiling broadly.

"Good to see you, Blue Hand. It's good to be back home. What's the word on the Res?"

"Nothing much, man. Just a few break-ins at the convenience store, kids trying to get ahold of the latest Iron Man comic books. Oh, and a murder," he said coyly.

"Murder? Where? Anyone I'd know?"

"Found the body a ways back at the Community Center. Guess it was the Preacher, or what was left of him. Seems a pack of wild dogs had at him. Pretty gruesome stuff."

"Any idea who did it?"

Blue Hand rubbed the gray stubble on his chin. "There's some say'n a young girl involved somehow. Guess she was doing some kind of art classes. She was lookin' at going off to college in some big city to study art. No one knows for sure. Not much to go on 'cept she went missing when it happened."

Jackson tried to hide his reaction to this news and asked to rent one of the old man's cars.

"Don't have any cash on me, but you can bill my grandfather."

Everyone knew Stone Wolf's grandfather was the wily old shaman and the man nodded his gray head without further discussion.

"He's good for it," he chuckled.

Jackson drove away from the airstrip in an old beater, but wasn't concerned about looks, just durability.

He made his way deeper into the Reservation territory and after an hour, rolled into his grandfather's drive.

The trailer Shadow Stalker lived in was as dated as the car parked off to the side. His grandfather always joked that relics were worth a lot, so his old truck was appreciating every year.

Jackson got out of the old Dodge just as his grandfather stepped onto the small porch of his trailer.

"Greetings to you, Stone Wolf," he called out, his face radiant with his love of his grandson.

"Grandfather, I am pleased to be back with you."

After a tight embrace, the two men went into the cool kitchen where Shadow Stalker had brewed a rich bodied tea and set out two mugs and a plate of Oreos.

"You were prepared for me I see, grandfather. And my favorite cookies," he said smiling into the flinty black eyes of the old man.

They sat and spoke of the clan and any changes in the old man's health. He seemed frailer to Jackson's eyes. Jackson knew the shaman was exerting his strength to maintain a connection to Little Bird.

"Grandfather, you know I must leave you soon to go to the hunter's lair. I ask your blessings upon my weapons and myself."

He laid out another hunting blade and a short ax, sharpened to a fine edge. The holy man held his hands over the two items and mouthed a silent prayer to bring them the blood of the enemy.

He turned to Jackson and laid his gnarled hands upon his shoulders and did the same for him.

Jackson left shortly after the blessings. The old man stood again on his small porch watching the broad back of his grandson as he walked back to the car. He felt the sun heating as it climbed higher into the cloudless skies, warming the soft breezes. Nevertheless, he shuddered as if blasted by a frigid wind out of the north.

As Jackson folded his long legs into the compact vehicle, the old man waved back at his outstretched hand. He purposely kept his recent vision of Little Bird to himself. While he could prevent her spirit from crossing over into the Hunter's darkness, he was unable to protect her body from being violated by the evil shaman, Dream Stalker.

He had unwillingly witnessed yet another seduction of the young woman by the man who had already captured her body's desires.

The shaman knew that Dream Stalker had his own visions and saw the beautiful Indian woman as soon as he ate the flesh of the wretch, Lionel Reed. The Hunter's shaman was driven to madness by his desire for the young beauty.

The old man left the sunny porch and returned to the tiny kitchen where he rinsed the mugs and returned them to the shelf. He tried to shake the vision of Tricia being manipulated so grievously by her own passions.

He was too old to see such things and experience a physical reaction. Yet, his scalp tingled as he tried to shut out the picture of Little Bird as she wrapped her legs around the huge Hunter.

"Do not be deceived by your passions, Little Bird," he spoke as he gazed out the small window above his sink. This man is a demon who seeks to destroy your soul forever. Ayo…he will possess more than your body then!"

Chapter 48

Jackson's travels had often taken him away from the home he knew since birth. The Reservation had changed little over time. He remembered the way to the old school grounds. A combination K trough 12, now converted to the large Community Center.

The Center housed a large Arts and Native Crafts Pavilion used by any tribe member and offering classes and studios to working artists and others studying native arts.

The rambling wood and brick one story structure faced the craggy blue stone of the mountain range, encircling it in a timeless embrace.

He pulled the small rental car into the still unpaved parking lot after looking around and smiling at old memories. Tricia would never have those memories again. The hard line of his jaw set at that thought.

Going directly to the semi-circle shaped desk just inside the door, he was warmly greeted by Joan Little Feather, still the receptionist after so many years.

"I can't believe these old eyes! Jackson Wolf," the diminutive woman said coming around her station to give him a quick hug as he leaned down.

Joan had been part of the original project team when they built the first school for their kids fifty years back. She was a well-respected Indian leader then and still wore that mantel in present day Res life.

At five foot nothing, Joan resembled her name, being slightly built, wearing her steel colored hair short and spikey. Jackson's grandfather used to joke how she closely resembled her hair.

"Joan, it's good to see you. I see you are still steering the Res ship. I'm impressed with the transformation of this old school building."

He was looking around, his eyes following the same hallway Tricia must have taken back to the studios, with her would-be attacker close behind. He tried to cover his frown by making a slow turn to look about.

After several minutes of exchanging brief stories, Jackson learned from her of the gruesome murder of the white preacher man. "It looked like a pack of wolves had eaten the body," she said looking away with a shudder.

Jackson let Joan continue to fill him in on local happenings to be polite, but was anxious to begin his search for the Hunter stronghold. He hoped he'd pick up some kind of intuitive clues by coming to the scene of the killing.

Leaving her after another ten minutes of chatting, he drove toward his clan's secure sweat lodge. He needed to undergo cleansing and spiritual renewal before his encounter with Dream Slayer, and would partake of the peyote mushroom. His grandfather had given his blessing to use this sacred method of vision-seeking for his search.

The humped profile of the lodge come into view. Jackson parked behind the squat structure, not wanting to raise curiosity about an unknown vehicle. He left all his newly blessed weapons inside the car and stripped down to his black briefs.

He pulled back the heavy deer skin flap that acted as a door and entered the circular holy site.

Standing still a moment, his eyes adjusted to the deep gloom created by a thick haze of steam that diffusing any light.

His grandfather had alerted Billy One Grass that his grandson would be doing a solo purification and seeking a vision during his sweat. All was in readiness for this quest. Though highly unusual, Billy knew better than to question the old shaman. Seeing the big Indian slip into the lodge he merely whispered his name by way of greeting.

"Stone Wolf."

Billy One Grass began to chant the prayers associated with a spirit cleansing rite as Jackson sat close to the heated stones. As an Elder of the clan, the chanting Indian had trained many years to conduct this purification ceremony.

He drizzled water over heated stones, carefully selected for this purpose, releasing clouds of steam into the confined space of the lodge.

Jackson sat erect, legs crossed, and translated the language of his Lakota forefathers in his head. The sweat began to gather and flow in rivulets from his body.

Help me, Father, to become pure of spirit before I send my voice to you. Help me in all that I am about to do.

The day faded outside the deer hide flap. The sky now held a blood-red sunset that hung ominously over the solitary form of the lodge.

Inside, Jackson was returning to his surroundings after a two hour vision journey. He had only ingested a small amount of the sacred peyote given to him by One Grass, but it was powerful and opened his mind's eye.

After a short rest to orient himself, Jackson unfolded his legs and pulled back the deer skin flap. He had not spoken a word since his arrival, and simply nodded at the solemn older man as he left.

The air was cooling now; a soft breeze stirred the damp hair clinging to his broad shoulders.

He moved toward the wide, fast-running stream adjacent to the sweat lodge. Breathing in deeply the chill that rode the night, he walked knee-deep into the brisk water and crouched down.

Five minutes later he stepped onto the bank. The droplets of water reflected the cold light of a full moon, hanging like a great yellow eye glaring down on a feeble earth.

He returned to the rental car, putting on a new set of clothes he took from his suitcase. He looked over at the other case on the back seat, Tricia's. He knew he had to find her soon. The vision was clear; the first night after the full moon, the Hunter's would hold the Blood Ritual. His love would be drained of her life's blood and given the dark blood of the possessed to drink.

She would be lost to the world of light.

The vision spoke the sacred name of the shaman, the fraud Bryce Powers. Dream Slayer. His evil, like his desire for Tricia was all-consuming.

Chapter 49

The location of the Hunter's enclave was revealed during Jackson's vision quest. As he drove over the rough, wind-swept roads, he reviewed what he had learned under the influence of the peyote.

The secretive clan had sought out a secluded part of the fabled Black Hills to carve out their headquarters. Jackson knew the Hunters were not the first Indians to move into the area; the region had seen the footprints of Native Americans for almost ten thousand years.

The pine-covered mountains, rising up from the plains spreading out like a blanket of brown and muted shades of green around their base, provided many places the break-away Hunters could hide from the Keepers.

Up until recent events, his grandfather had been willing to leave them unnoticed and unchallenged. The death of the white Preacher changed all of that.

Jackson was headed to one of the more remote parts of the dense forests, above the northern-most part of the Reservation.

Over a century ago, the whites had established a bustling town in the area, but predictably, when the gold petered out, they uprooted, leaving a rotting ghost town to the mercies of nature in their wake.

His drive would be over an hour to the isolated area. The moon seemed to race along just ahead of him while he followed the track of paved and graveled roads.

His mind kept wandering back to the sweat lodge and his vision quest.

He had clearly seen Little Bird lying upon a round bed covered in wolf furs. She was sleeping, but he knew her spirit was not peaceful and she found no rest.

As he watched her through this mental connection, a shadow suddenly hung over her still form. It lingered there several minutes, covering her body in her vulnerable state.

Jackson remembered how he tried to call out to her, but couldn't penetrate a heavy layer of dark magic that had been placed around her. His hands gripped the wheel tightly.

His grandfather had instructed One Grass to help prepare Jackson for the journey ahead. Before he drove away, the old man handed him a heavy leather jacket lined in sheep wool. Jackson glanced over at it now as he headed toward his enemy stronghold set deep in the pine forests of the Black Hills.

There were no other vehicles on the narrow roadways as he pressed his small car into the curves like a race car driver. He hadn't slept in over 24 hours and thought he was hallucinating when he saw lights moving through the woods to his right, mid-way up the rugged mountain base. Quickly shutting off his headlights, he cut the engine, letting the car drift over to the berm of the roughly graveled road.

He knew there were no small villages scattered this far north of the main Reservation. Counting, he made out six lights, likely torches, moving steadily upward through the woods.

"This must be it," he whispered into the stillness. Only the ticking of the cooling engine answered him.

The progress of the small column seemed slow, indicating primitive pathways were being followed. *Likely kept that way so no attention will be drawn to their existence,* Jackson surmised, watching them as they snaked their way higher onto the side of the mountain.

Jackson reached behind him for the heavy coat. Getting into it, he was already grateful for its warmth since he had to turn off the engine, losing his heat source.

He took the two knives and the short ax out of a leather bag and got out of the car. Standing on the side of the road, he slipped a blade into his boot and slipped the sacred knife into a beaded scabbard hanging from his belt. He wrapped a small strip of leather around the short ax and put it at his back. The cold blade lay against his shirt on the right side.

He was ready.

The thick scent of pine smothered any other as he began his ascent. All he heard in the darkness was the low moan of the wind through the feathery branches of the trees and the steady beat of his heart.

Jackson was a superb tracker, but the Hunters hadn't bothered to cover their route. At one point Jackson stopped moving and listened. The wind was stronger as he went further up the mountain and it carried a different sound now, the sound of voices, soft as the burble of a brook, but still discernable to his ear as human.

Must be the band I'm following. He figured they felt comfortable enough to speak to one another, so were getting closer to their campsite and were more relaxed. *Good. They will let their guard down now that they are closer to their clan.*

Jackson didn't want to assume his Keeper form just yet, even though the Hunters would have sentries around the perimeter of the site. He didn't need to waste any energy on the transformation. He would simply dispatch them using stealth and his blessed weapons.

He slowed his own progress, not wanting to overtake the small group. Their voices were muted by the heavy woods and distorted by the wind, but he picked out a few words. "The woman . . .

dangerous . . . her here!" These sounded angry and were tinged with concern.

Jackson smiled tightly, figuring out the missing words. He now was sure not all of the Hunters were happy with their shaman bringing Tricia among them. Jackson knew that the Blood Ritual was not for a shaman's sexual pleasure alone. It was supposed to be shared in part by the clan, to bring them all more strength and powers.

Obviously, their shaman had a different plan. The power would be his, just as the woman would be his, and his alone.

Crouching down behind a large moss-covered boulder, Jackson tried to pick up on more of the random comments. Instead, he watched as the torches were swallowed by the darkness one by one. He knew the Hunters must have entered some kind of structure, or cave. Their shaman would be aware of their return.

Jackson waited until he saw the last glow disappear, certain they were all back inside the compound. He would make his move as Shadow Stalker had instructed. Until then, he would reach for the spiritual tether between him and his grandfather. Then, he would once more give over his body and spirit to the transformation, to become Keeper of The People.

Chapter 50

The wind rattled through the braches of the thick pines, an unseen force causing them to quake in its passing. Jackson was crouched beside the boulder when the last glow of torchlight was snuffed out. He began to whisper the sacred words that would connect him through his spirit, directly to his grandfather, Shadow Stalker. The ripple of power in the air began to distort the space around him. Filtered moonlight showed the trees and boulder shimmering like reflections on a stirred pond.

Jackson would not transform until the last possible moment, conserving that energy carefully. There were at least seven Hunters to deal with, including their shaman, Dream Slayer. He hoped to take out the six warriors before he had to face their leader. He stepped away from the rock, slipping the knife out of the sheath at his side and began to climb.

There were many old mines in this area of the Reservation, left by the gold-crazed white men. They tore at the mountain's heart in their frenzy to make a big strike. Jackson figured the Hunters likely hid away in one of these forgotten holes in the granite and earth.

He stopped after a short time, kneeling down to search for signs of the Hunters among the pine needles and trampled grasses. He was rewarded on his third attempt. The six had clearly passed through the area and were headed up toward a less dense patch of trees.

His keen hearing picked up a rustling sound off to his right as he was about to stand. He froze, gripping his knife and studying the shadows around him.

Nothing moved.

He had already noticed that there were none of the usual noises of the woods at night, no night birds calling, no nocturnal animals skittering through the dark, searching for prey. The forest felt unnatural and strange as he passed through it.

There was another muted sound. This time it was accompanied by the heavy musk scent. *They left one of their group to guard the entrance. I must be close.*

The Hunter was waiting for him to give away his position by moving. Jackson knew he couldn't win a fight if the other had shifted, but he didn't want to tap into his powers yet. He reached down with his free hand, feeling around until he found a large rock. Still kneeling, he tossed it into a small clearing just ahead of his hiding place, hoping to come up behind his enemy.

There was another muffled sound, only this time from where the rock had landed. Jackson reached behind and pulled the short ax from his belt. He moved toward what he hoped was the Hunter's exposed flank. He crept a few steps before seeing a large form materialize in the gloom.

Lunging like a diver into deep waters, Jackson hit his enemy squarely in the back, driving his long blade deeply, severing the spinal cord. The Hunter never uttered a sound.

It was over in less than a minute. Jackson stood panting. The light from the hazy moon glinted off the blood spatter covering the ground and lower tree limbs. As he watched, the body vanished, claimed by the clan's Spirit Taker.

Jackson was certain this was the only guard he'd encounter because the clan would need its members to conduct the Drinking Blood Ritual.

Jackson felt a tremor go through him as Shadow Stalker's deep voice describing the ritual that lay ahead for Little Bird. He spoke this to him while the peyote still crystalized and held sway over his consciousness and opened his inner sight. *They induce a deep sleep upon their victim, a dreamless state where they can speak and their bodies can respond to all they undergo in the ceremony. This is so they can beg and cry out. When they have been secured to the shaman's satisfaction, he will command all his followers to kneel in a circle around the Blood Stone. He will chant his prayers to the Dark One, beckoning him to come forward. He invites his Dark master to take possession of him, to carry out the rest of the ritual using the shaman's body as an instrument of terror and pain. This is what awaits Little Bird, Stone Wolf. But for her, there will be no release of her body to death. She will be mated to Dream Slayer and remain at his side into the time without time.*

The reality of what Tricia would suffer if he failed was almost overwhelming. He consciously ended the link to his grandfather until he had collected himself. He moved forward, keeping close to the ground, the sharp smell of the pine needles giving some cleansing comfort to his senses.

A humped shape loomed out of the darkness, outlined against the night sky. Jackson concluded this was a man-made structure. The shape led him to believe it was some kind of meeting lodge for the Hunters.

He approached soundlessly, watching for any other guards.

He still waited to make his transformation, wanting to use all his human skills before he made contact with the Hunters and especially their leader.

As he studied the large structure, he saw faint stripes of light showing through gapes and openings in the roofing. A picture of those torches he had seen earlier on the mountain trail flashed through his mind.

Off to his right, there was a larger swath of light falling on well-used ground. He had found the entrance to the lodge.

Before he moved forward, he slipped out of his borrowed jacket and hung it carefully from a low branch. From a distance it looked like the silhouette of a man.

Approaching the entryway from the side, Jackson saw it had been left unguarded. He moved a heavy buffalo skin aside a crack to look in. It was as he imagined, primitive and ripe with the pungent odor of an animal's lair. Torches, thrust into holders made from deer or elk antlers, marked the way leading deeper into the oblong wooden and dirt structure.

Jackson could make out a few details of his surroundings when he moved the heavy flap and slid inside. The forward part of the lodge was filled with various sized drums, rattles, skulls and animal skins. It was the skulls that immediately captured Jackson's attention. Among the common coyote, buffalo and wolf, were two human heads, the skin and hair still intact, likely preserved for a ritual. They were skewered by short poles, then stuck into holes drilled into a pine log. Jackson wondered if they were made ready for burning that way.

He knew they both were Indians. Jackson grimaced when he recognized the older looking one.

Joseph Two Clouds, Joey Banks, the Lakota Keeper who went missing from Chicago a few months back after starting a private investigation into illegal drugs.

He suspected the other skull belonged to the runaway boy he had failed to find on that earlier assignment. He gritted his teeth and silently swore to avenge them both. He studied the stern look on the older man's desiccated face, a face that had become his death mask. This Keeper had lost his life and powers right here in this lodge. *Probably met Bryce Powers same way we did, while he was trolling for his next victim,* he thought grimly.

The long room was divided by a floor to ceiling curtain made from several wolf skins. Their beautiful fur looked inviting to the touch in the soft glow of torch-light. One of the pelts still had the wolf's noble head attached. Its glassy golden eyes seemed to be watching Jackson, communicating a tale of terrible death.

Jackson rubbed the back of his hand where the tattoo wolf in inky profile, rippled slightly under his skin. He could sense movement on the other side of the fur panel and quickly hid himself in the shadows, crouching low behind the crowded rack of skulls.

Suddenly, the furs were pulled aside and an Indian, the size of the fabled Goliath, stood within touching distance of Jackson's hiding place.

He was naked save for a leather loin cloth. His dark red skin was smeared in some kind of oil, highlighting the bulked up muscles of his limbs and massive chest. Jackson was barely breathing, not wanting to take on this brute without the benefit of transforming into his Keeper form. That would be a fight he'd likely lose to the bigger man.

The Indian scanned the outer room carefully before moving, giving Jackson an opportunity to get a glimpse into what he figured was the ceremonial room.

He spotted four other Hunters, but knew there were at least two more who trekked up the side of the mountain. The big Indian dropped the curtain and moved over to the drums and rattles. Picking up a large drum and several rattles in his huge hands, he moved the heavy curtain aside once more, letting it drop behind him in a wash of stale air.

Jackson took a deep breath. His next move had to put him inside the ceremonial room.

He would have to wait until Tricia was actually on the ritual stone before he could make a move, but he needed to get inside the inner sanctum first.

Just as he was about to leave his hiding place, the door flap was moved from outside, a burst of smoky moonlight illuminating the dark recesses where Jackson hunkered down.

Another Indian stepped quietly into the room. He was much smaller than Goliath and seemed unfamiliar with the surroundings. As he squatted down lower, Jackson heard a small, clear voice. "Stone Wolf. I am here."

Chapter 51

Jackson immediately sprang to his feet. "Grandfather," he whispered when he was beside him.

"We must hurry, my son. The ceremony has begun and Little Bird will soon be brought here by their leader."

Jackson didn't question, knowing the powerful Shaman, Shadow Stalker, had used his vision-making peyote to clarify their next actions. The old man had brought his Spirit Robe, made from the hide of the great White Buffalo and passed down through generations of shamans who had served the Keepers.

"We shall enter their ceremonial circle with the weight of the Protector of the Keepers around us." With that, he easily swung the heavy robe, covering the two of them from head to toe. The robe had yellowed with age, but still retained its potent power and the two men seemed swallowed into its inner space.

Moving as one, they pulled the wolf pelts aside and stepped into the ceremonial room.

Jackson counted seven Hunters, forming a wide circle around a flat-topped boulder. The original stone had turned blackish with the staining of centuries of use, especially in the smooth surface where the victims would be laid out.

He guessed this was their Blood Stone. He confirmed this when he scanned it further and noted the small pots set at intervals to catch the blood of their next victim.

The Drinking Blood ritual was staged and only needed Tricia to begin.

This part of the wood and mud building was nearly as hot as a sweat lodge. Jackson noticed all the Hunters were stripped down to a leather loin cloth. A sweet smell of sandalwood incense burning somewhere, mixed in with the sour smell of sweating men.

Jackson felt his grandfather nudge him lightly and followed his gaze to the rear of the room. Evidently there was another entrance into the ceremonial chamber.

Suddenly, the man he'd known as Bryce Powers stood among them in his true persona, the shaman, Dream Slayer.

Like the others, he was stripped to a loin cloth. As he entered the circle of men, Jackson saw one of the Hunters bring something to the Shaman. He stepped behind Dream Slayer, placing the head of a once magnificent wolf, like a crown, upon the gleaming black hair of his powerful leader.

The wolf's pelt was still attached, its extraordinary size indicating an Alpha male. Dream Slayer pulled the thick, silvery fur around himself like a royal mantle, ignoring the steamy atmosphere of the room. He signaled to the man.

The Hunter turned, melting into the gloom behind him.

A minute passed in frozen silence.

The deep hush was shattered as a burst of throbbing drum beats stirred the air with reverberation. The rhythm was slow at first, but as the shaman turned toward the hidden entryway, they grew frenzied.

The Hunters all turned now as the door opened and Tricia walked in. The drumming ceased.

She had a blank expression on her face, her eyes unfocused and staring.

She's been drugged Jackson thought. With his strong connection to his grandfather, his thoughts were heard and the old man nodded.

She wore a traditional bridal dress, made from snowy-white buckskin, coming to her knees and finished with a fringe of long leather strips matching the fringe on both arms. There was intricate bead work across the bodice and intertwined with a row of leather fringe just under the breast. Her slender waist was emphasized by a snug fitting beaded belt matching the bead work throughout.

Jackson's breath caught in his throat as he saw this beautiful woman standing only a few feet away.

Like the others, she never looked in the direction where Jackson huddled beside his grandfather under the Spirit Robe.

Dream Slayer's chest seemed to expand in a possessive pride as he looked around at his clansmen and saw the lust in each of their eyes.

Tricia began to move toward the wolf-clad shaman. The soft scuffing of her moccasins made Jackson wince as she made her way to the other man's open arms.

When she stood before him, Dream Slayer reached out to gently stroke her upturned face. Tricia had no reaction to his touch except a slight fluttering of her eyes as if she struggled to wake herself from a bad dream.

Every muscle in Jackson's body strained to explode into action.

His grandfather gently laid a restraining hand on his arm. *You must wait. It will be soon,* he warned sternly with his eyes and the pressure of his gnarled hand.

Dream Slayer moved behind the still form of the beautiful woman. In the dim lighting from the torches, there was a quicksilver gleam as a long thin blade appeared in his hand.

Jackson's body screamed for release as he watched the shaman carefully use the blade to cut through each of the fasteners at the back of the dress. With her arms held straight to her sides, the heavy garment slipped to the floor and she stood naked except for a brief loin cloth similar to the men's. Her breasts were covered in intricate painted symbols.

Without speaking a word, the shaman took Tricia's hand and led her to the three steps at the side of the Blood Stone. Her eyes still held their unfocused glaze when she ascended to the wide ledge surrounding the blood-tainted rock.

Dream Slayer followed her and when he too stood on the flat rim, he took her hand once more and helped her lay down on the unyielding stone. She had no reaction as her warm body made contact with its cold surface, except to immediately close her eyes as if to sleep.

There was a marked arousal in the Hunters that had been watching the proceedings with rapt attention. They had become more animated and some began to make strange animal noises.

The shaman ignored the rising excitement.

Just as the guttural sounds were becoming more and more pronounced among the Hunters, their shaman called in the deep, sensual voice Jackson remembered of the cowboy, Bryce Powers.

"It is time! You will feed on life and know power in your true form!"

There was a roar from the Hunters, as each of them fell to their knees, muscled bodies slick with sweat. Their bodies twisted into distorted positions, backs humped, arms and legs elongated. Soon, they all resembles nothing less than the monsters from the folk tales told by the ancient ones of the tribe.

While the seven Hunters were transforming from their human state into the creatures of the Dark, their shaman had returned his attention to the vulnerable woman.

"Little Bird, this night you become one with me."

He stroked the fine curve of her cheek bone, his finger trailing down to her jaw and on to the steady pulse in her delicate neck.

Jackson's grandfather reached out to grab his forearm and squeezed it to help steady him. He looked into Jackson's face and let him hear his words.

"We must leave our bodies now and bring out our spirit warriors, Stone Wolf. Are you ready?"

Without speaking, Jackson crouched down on one knee beneath the Spirit Robe. He felt a surge of energy rip through his body like liquid fire, searing his nerve endings until they were enflamed within contorting muscle and bone. His flesh became distended and sprouted a heavy coat of fur. In this form, his every action was ruled by the spirit warrior who possessed his body.

While he went through his transformation, so too had his grandfather, Shadow Stalker. His spirit warrior had changed his grizzled, gnarled body until he became as fierce and powerful as the white buffalo that called him brother.

The growls and quick snapping of jaws among the Hunters was Dream Slayer's signal to begin the Ritual of Blood.

Chapter 52

Tricia's eyes flew open. Dream Slayer was using the long blade of his knife to trace the intricate symbols painted on her breasts. There was a deeply satisfied look on his lean face as he looked into the terror-filled eyes of the young woman.

He leaned over her, his lips inches from her face.

"You can't move Little Bird, so don't tire yourself by trying. We have a long night ahead of us."

The seven Hunters had all moved closer to the Blood Rock in anticipation of the first bloodletting. Their long, tooth-filled snouts were spattered with thick gobs of saliva, hungry for the first taste.

Tricia was paralyzed by the drug the shaman had given her earlier. At the same time, it heightened every touch and breath of air upon her naked skin. The shaman wanted her pain to be intensified by her inability to escape or even fight against what was happening to her.

Dream Slayer brushed her lips with the knife and then pressed his mouth over hers in a hard, biting kiss. When he stood back up, the Hunters went wild as he showed the blood he had drawn from the delicate flesh.

Tricia watched his face as he turned his attention back to her supine body. He had a wide grin on his bloody lips. Clearly he was enjoying her terror. His knife flashed with the glint of firelight off its sharp blade. She struggled to move, to will her body to roll away. The knife arced above her and sliced into her right arm, making a small, but deep cut. She was unable to even pull her arm away as her warm blood began to drip from the open wound. Her eyes widened slightly as he opened the left arm the same way, using a deft stroke of the now bloodied knife. Her muscles may be numb, but her nerve endings sent clear messages of pain to her foggy brain. Tricia screamed, discovering that her vocal chords weren't paralyzed. Soon the lodge was filled with her outrage and pain.

Dream Slayer went about his work like a trained surgeon, not cutting enough to kill her, but releasing a free flow of blood from her extremities. The agony of the screaming girl brought the Hunters into a frenzy. They fought each other over the slowly filling bowls of fresh blood, often drawing blood from other Hunters in the clashing of claws and teeth.

The mayhem was all Shadow Stalker and Stone Wolf needed to make their appearance among the blood-crazed brutes. They each came from behind a demented Hunter and with the efficiency of trained killers, sliced open the throats of both. Giving them a shove to place them back among their slavering fellow Hunters, they turned the pack into piranha devouring an injured swimmer.

The grotesque forms, seen in the wavering light from the torches, immediately began tearing into the bodies before they returned to their human form and what was left was gathered by their Spirit Taker.

There was no interference on the part of their shaman as he had become enflamed to the point of madness by the sight of the moaning girl. The bloodletting had been restricted to cuts on her arms and legs, but now he stared at her exposed breasts with a renewed hunger. With a swift movement he slashed the bloody knife just under her left breast. Her scream brought a snake-like smile to his face as he leaned over and began licking the new gash as it bled freely.

He tore off her loin cloth, then his own and was about to enter her when he was suddenly airborne. Stone Wolf had launched himself over the bodies of two other Hunters he had just destroyed. The last three fought savagely over the blood dripping into the bowls. None saw the huge wolf-like creature, or cared. Hearing Tricia's sobs and screams kept them in a state of turmoil.

Dream Slayer landed under the weight of his attacker, his back crashing into the drums and bowls of incense. He hadn't transformed yet, because he wanted to take Tricia again. Making her bleed for his clan while they watched him mount her would be the highlight of the ritual making her his bride.

Stone Wolf was out of his mind with hatred of the large Indian lying beneath him. His knife was ready to plunge into his throat when he was attacked by the beast he called Goliath. The massive arms wrapped around him, pressing out all the air from his lungs and threatening to collapse them. Stone Wolf threw his head back and smashed it into the giant's wide nose. He heard a crack. It was enough to loosen the death grip on him and he bounded away in a blur of speed. Though he was able to fight off his attacker, Stone Wolf still had to destroy the shaman and he needed to do it before he made the transformation.

Dream Slayer pulled himself up by using the side of the flat rock. It was now getting slick with the blood flowing freely from the many slashes over Tricia's body.

Shadow Stalker used the distraction of the blood to kill the two remaining Hunters, taking them from behind while they lapped up the overflowing bowls of blood. Their Spirit Taker removed their bodies within five of his own heartbeats.

He knew he had depleted his own physical resources by then and retreated to a dark corner of the lodge to make his change back to human form. While he began to feel the slackening of taught muscle and the sloughing off of thick fur, he was at his most vulnerable.

This is how Goliath found him.

The massive Indian was armed now with a heavy club, studded with sharp metal points. Swinging his brawny arms in a wide arc, he caught the transforming shaman in the back of his skull. It caved in like a dropped melon, spilling brain matter. The incredible force of the hit detached the head in a fountain of blood.

Stone Wolf was jolted as his connection with his grandfather was suddenly severed. He staggered away from Dream Slayer and would have reverted to his human form, but for a moan from the top of the bloodied rock.

The Hunters were only two now. The Shaman, Dream Slayer and his giant. Both were coming slowly toward the Keeper, eyes full of death. The shaman had not taken his creature form for some reason and he called over to the lone Keeper.

"You are at a disadvantage, Stone Wolf. It seems the old shaman, Shadow Stalker, is no more than an empty husk after all.

Little Bird needs to be healed quickly, or as you can see, she will bleed to death. Only I can bring about that healing, Keeper. She belongs to me now and will serve me as my mate. I will allow you a few more minutes of life while I show you my power over her life and death."

He turned away from the Keeper, leaving Goliath to watch him for any attempt to interfere. Reaching out to Tricia, he placed his hands over her, moving from her neck down to her feet. As he did, the oozing slashes across her flesh, began to close off and seal, the skin unmarked and supple looking. When he had finished he glanced over at the crouched form of the Keeper and shouted to his giant, "Now!"

The monster raised the bloody club, gray fur and gray matter sticking to the spikes. Stone Wolf sprang to the side to avoid the sweep of the powerful swing and then slashed the giants back, exposing the spine. The huge Indian howled in pain and fell to his knees. The Keeper lunged for his exposed throat and with another swipe of sharp claws, ripped his head from his heaving shoulders.

Suddenly there was dead silence in the lodge.

It was time to deal with the shaman and Stone Wolf began his change back to his human form. He felt the twisted bone and muscle take shape and within a minute, he stood naked, shinning like an ancient warrior-god in the low torch light.

Chapter 53

The Shaman, Dream Slayer, looked stunned for a moment as he saw his giant killer fall to his knees, followed by his decapitation. He held the ceremonial bloodletting knife in his hand, turning his eyes downward at the half-dead girl. His face showed a conflict of emotions as he considered driving the sharp point into her beating heart. His enflamed desire for her stayed his hand and instead he leapt the three feet from the Blood Stone.

The Spirit Takers had already gathered the last of the Hunters. He now stood alone to face the Keeper, Jackson Wolf.

"I will allow you to live, Keeper, if you leave here now. You have shown your courage in battle and I will honor you with your life."

Jackson stood several feet away, his jaw tightly set, eyes flashing the rage he felt toward the shaman. The long blade in his hand was dripping with his last kill.

"Here is where we end it, Dream Slayer. Your life will be returned to the evil ones who gather the spirits of the fallen Hunters." While he spoke, he slowly moved to his right, Dream Slayer following with his eyes. It was an old ploy, but Jackson knew the shaman would watch his every move closely and he used that focus to get him off balance.

The shaman had been holding the long knife at his side, but now brought it up to waist level. "She can never be yours, Stone Wolf. You know that. I have marked her with my brand," he called over to the shifting Keeper.

"I have seen the bleeding moon, but it is no more. Shadow Stalker reclaimed the pure spirit of Little Bird as his last act. See for yourself."

"What is this? Do you still dream, Keeper?" he sneered.

He nevertheless positioned himself slightly, surprised to see the figure of his intended bride sitting up from her hard bed.

Using this distraction, Jackson launched himself at the shaman, bringing him to the ground. Though caught off guard, Dream Slayer lashed out with a powerful blow to Jackson's arm, causing his weapon to be flung a few feet away.

The shaman was quick to use his superior strength to roll over and pin Jackson beneath him, restraining him with an arm across his throat and grabbing for a knife off the bloodied floor. He raised the knife to plunge its long blade up and under the heaving rib cage, when his blood-stained hand began to tremble. His fingers lost their strength, becoming gnarled and veiny. The knife dropped from his grip. His handsome face distorted with a stricken look as he tried to understand what had happened.

Jackson pushed hard and rolled the stricken Hunter beneath him. He reached out to his own fallen knife. It sprang like a magnet to a steel hand.

With a single, almost graceful movement, the knife found its mark and the shaman's feeble struggles ended.

Jackson panted.

"Thank you, grandfather."

He knew this was Shadow Stalker's knife and it was spelled to serve no other, except the grandson he would protect even in death.

Jackson sprang to his feet as the shaman's body was claimed by the dark Spirit Takers. He felt the chill of their presence as they moved like a bitter wind to reclaim the fallen.

His attention was brought back by a small voice, nearly inaudible from its long silence.

"Ja…Jack."

Before she might faint and her head smash against the hard surface, Jackson leapt onto the flat stone, catching her up in his arms. He was holding her to his chest, speaking softly, calming her fears with his words. Carrying her down the three steps from the Blood Rock, he slowly made his way out of the lodge.

The cool night air revived Tricia enough to smile weakly at the concerned face of her love.

"You came for me," was all she murmured before closing her eyes and pressing closer to his naked chest.

It took a long time, going slowly to avoid pitfalls hidden among the shadows and rocks, before they came down the side of the mountain. Jackson breathed an exhausted sigh of relief when the road and the old car came into view. He opened the front door and gently sat Tricia down. Her eyes flickered open for a second and immediately closed as she drifted off.

Jackson suspected the heavy doses of drugs she'd been given still had some effect on her.

He slipped her arms into the jacket he had grabbed off the tree limb on his way back, closing the snaps against the cold. There was an old Army blanket in the back seat of the car which he used to cover her bare legs.

Before the blanket was laid across her lap, Jackson noticed that the long slash marks inflicted upon her flesh had begun to fade. Some reverted back to her smooth, creamy copper skin as he watched.

Speaking to her softly, even if she couldn't hear, Jackson said, "The great Shaman, Shadow Stalker watches over you still, Little Bird."

He smiled to himself, feeling safe but sad, and started the car for their long drive ahead.

His plan was to stop at a small motel along the road where they could both shower and change into fresh clothes. They would leave for the airport early in the morning. He had sent a text message to Angie and Teddy to meet them at Midway Airport and give them a lift home.

He considered that strange concept . . . home. Not the densely wooded mountains around the Reservation, but a teaming, concrete mecca, Chicago. He looked over at Tricia, her lovely face relaxed in a peaceful sleep at last.

"It's time for us to go home, Little Bird," he whispered.

The glow from the dashboard softened the interior of the car, making Jackson feel like they traveled with the spirit of Shadow Stalker.

"Grandfather," he whispered. The crunch of the gravel beneath his tires, the only response.

Chapter 54

Tricia was deep in thought when he stepped onto the spacious balcony of their condo. She was sitting with her long legs drawn up to her chest, her arms wrapped around them and staring into the woods surrounding the complex.

They had been able to buy the newly built home with money Jack had transferred upon arriving back in Chicago. He explained the money was from his share of profits from several gambling properties he had interests in through the tribe.

Tricia didn't question this, but hated to be what she called a kept woman. He always answered with a smile and his typical response.

"Don't be silly, love. What I have is ours, not mine. Let's just enjoy it together."

They moved away from the city into a suburb called Pine Grove as soon as Tricia felt strong enough. Neither of them wanted to be anywhere that could conjure memories of Bryce Powers, or the Hunters.

During the interim period, before renting the condo, Jackson had insisted they move into another empty flat in the same building. The land lord, Harold, was more than happy to accommodate their request when Jackson offered him twice the rent.

'"We'll only be here for a few more months, Harold, and then we're out of here."

Within a month they had located their new condo and with help from Angie and Teddy, they made an easy move of their few personal items.

While she didn't show any outward scars from her horrific near-death experience at the hands of Dream Slayer, Jackson knew Tricia needed a new environment to fully recover her spirits.

Their new home was a forty-five minute drive from the outskirts of downtown Chicago. This meant their friends were still within visiting distance. They had become closer to the young couple over the months before the move, but the topic of Bryce Powers and the creatures he controlled was only mentioned once.

Over pizza and a second bottle of wine, the relaxed atmosphere became tense when Tricia blurted out "I'm OK, guys. I feel like you're kind of tip-toeing around what happened to me."

Angie reached across the pizza box and grabbed Tricia's hand.

"We're just so happy you're safe Trish! Teddy and I know there was a lot of weird shit going down with that rich creep, but we don't need particulars unless you need to share them. Remember, girl, we have our own paranormal bull twicky to wrap our heads around!"

This took down the elephant in the room to a manageable size and they all shared small, but significant experiences. Tricia left out the sexual encounters she experienced, not wanting any living person to ever hear how she felt both revulsion and desire during each of them.

Though they called often, their friend's visits back and forth to the condo had become fewer over time, until most of their interaction was via text messaging and a rare dinner in Chicago.

Jackson saw the loneliness written clearly on Tricia's face.

"What are you thinking so hard about, love?" Jackson asked, placing his warm hand on her shoulder.

"I was looking at the trees and listening," she answered smiling up at him and squeezing his hand.

Her smile held the love she felt for him, but couldn't conceal the hint of sadness he saw there too. "Can you tell me what's wrong, Trish? I can read it in your eyes." He took a deep breath when she didn't answer right away, looking down at her lap. "You're not happy here are you?" It was more of a statement than a question. He'd already guessed at the reason for her moody glances into the woods and her long silences. Their love making was just as satisfying as before the Blood Ritual, but even then, he felt her holding back a part of herself that she'd always opened to him. He sat in the chair next to her and reached for her hands as she lowered her legs to face him.

"I think of home and I can't help feeling lonely, Jack. I know we can't go back, but I know my parents must be crazy with worry for me. And after what happened to, to him, everyone must have guessed I had something to do with the murder."

"Tricia, it wasn't murder! You were defending yourself from a vicious attack by a depraved man. Look, if you want to go back to the Res, we will. I can arrange for a private reunion with your folks and keep our visit secret from the elders and the rest of the people."

She searched his dark eyes closely. "Seriously? You can do that? I just want to see them to explain what happened and why I had to run away. I know they wouldn't worry and wonder then."

Jackson leaned in to brush her cheek where I sun touched it, turning her skin a burnished copper, soft and rich. "We can leave here as soon as I make our plans. I'll need to get word to your parents and be sure they don't tell anyone else in the family. I'll do that today."

He reached over and pulled her head close to his, kissing her warm mouth. He couldn't break off from that kiss. It seemed like a dam had collapsed around them and they became swept away with their desires.

Jackson brought her to her feet. He picked her up and carried her back through the open sliding glass door and through to their bedroom.

This time their coupling was like a long symphony, rising, building and suddenly, bursting into a crescendo of passion. They laid upon the covers exhausted and panting, but smiling at each other like coconspirators in the perfect crime.

The next morning Jackson placed the call to Tricia's parents.

He had to wait until they stopped screaming questions into the phone and crying out her name over and over, before he could lay out his careful plan. They understood that her visit with them would need to be totally undetected by everyone, including aunts, uncles, cousins and especially, Tribal Elders.

"We will only be with you a short time because of the risk, but if you follow my plan that will allow you at least two hours for your visit," he was telling them.

They were quick to agree and over-joyed with the prospect of seeing their daughter. "It's been almost a year." Her mother was sobbing. "But we are grateful to you for whatever time we can have with our Little Bird."

His cell phone went flying out of his hand and onto the bed as Tricia launched herself into his arms. He finally saw the spark that had been missing for so long shinning from her eyes. Tears streamed down her face and for once, he felt them cleanse her spirit.

Chapter 55

Her parents easily found the roadside café described by Jackson. They sat sipping coffees when the handsome Indian walked up to their table.

"Mr. and Mrs. Cooley? I'm Jackson Wolf. You know of my grandfather I'm sure. He was The People's Shaman, Shadow Stalker."

They both looked stunned with this introduction, holding their mugs half-way to open mouths. The father recovered himself first. "You are Stone Wolf, then?" he asked with a tinge of awe in his words.

Jackson joined them at the table to review the plan he'd devised for them to visit with their daughter. The couple left the café shortly after he threw ten dollars down on the table and headed out the door.

 He checked the rear view mirror to be sure they followed and headed toward his grandfather's lodge. It was in a rugged area of woodland at the base of the mountains, a good distance from the main Reservation community.

They would leave their cars hidden in a lean-to built for that purpose, hiking deeper into the woods for about fifteen minutes. They had dressed for this trek following his instructions on the phone. The Keepers had used this remote place for hundreds of years, building and rebuilding it as needed. Jackson felt secure in bringing Tricia's parents there, knowing they respected the old ways of the Tribe and the Elders.

In the pre-dawn hours, Jackson made the long drive with Tricia after flying in on a red-eye flight from Chicago.

Armed with a thermos of coffee and a few breakfast muffins, she found herself in a mound-shaped building, with mud-daubed walls and intertwined tree branches forming perfect camouflage for the low roof.

It was used by him and his grandfather on many nights of hard training in the mystical powers he would need as a Keeper of The People.

Tricia's curiosity had her walking around outside of the primitive-looking building for nearly an hour. She loved the woods and the clean smell of pine and earth. She returned to the lodge long enough to get some coffee to ward off the morning chill.

Jackson had told her it would be at least two hours before he returned with her parents. A false twilight colored the woods as the sun struggled weakly to penetrate the heavy branches. The shadowing created a kind of denseness in the air around her.

She hadn't bothered lighting the candles Jackson showed her earlier, thinking that being in the open would be preferable to the ancient smells radiating from the interior of the lodge. Taking the steaming mug with her, she found a seat on a tree stump near the cabin. She was thinking about the coming reunion with her parents when she heard something moving through the underbrush.

A chill ran down her spine.

Jumping off her perch, she sprinted for the rude shelter. She threw the lock into place, but it seemed as flimsy as the rest of the lodge. It was merely a sliding bolt, barely hanging onto the time-warped wood frame.

She backed away from the door into the darkest recesses of the long room. The back of her knees came into contact with the assortment of ceremonial drums, rattles, and ankle bells, lining the wall in mute harmony.

Desperate to find a weapon of some kind, she spotted several bone-handle knives, pierced through with leather thongs decorated in colorful feathers. She grabbed two off the pegs where they hung, studying their condition. They seemed freshly honed.

Standing with a knife in each hand, she felt better prepared. If it was just an animal, she'd be safe enough inside the cabin. If it was a man…

Her hands clenched around the bone handles.

It took all of her will power not to succumb to the fear that began to gnaw at her gut. She pressed against the rough walls of the cabin in an attempt to quell her shaking. Her heart was hammering in her chest like one of the drums at her feet.

Trying to penetrate the gloom for somewhere to hide, she made out the huge bear hide she'd seen earlier, stretched out on the back wall.

Tricia quickly got behind the massive black hide. She was immediately smothered in the heavy scent coming off the old pelt. It was like smoke from a campfire, mixed with earth and rotting vegetation. She took small gulps of air through her mouth. When she heard the door rattle, she held her breath altogether.

The natural sounds of early morning in the woods were muffled behind the heavy fur of the stretched bear skin. Then, even in the complete darkness of her hiding place, she heard a strange, piercing bird call, to be answered moments later from further away with the same eerie trilling. These calls were followed by something slapping hard against the door.

The old wood rattled in its frame. Her body went stiff with fear as she waited for the intruder to smash through the weak barrier.

She squeezed her eyes shut, trying to steel herself to confront whatever was out there.

A darker panic began to settle around her in the cloying confines of the bear's fur. Without warning, she felt the bear skin begin to stir around her where it pressed heavily upon her body.

Her eyes flew open. There was a vague light radiating from the knives she held. She had no time to react.

The flimsy door crashed onto the floor and two Hunters loped into the lodge.

The Hunters stood in the middle of the room. Both had transformed to their creature state. Their long snouts nuzzled the thick air of the room, tasting it for their quarry. They turned as one toward the back wall, and found their prey.

Their curved backs rippled with muscle under a thick mating of black-brown fur. The ends of splayed fingers were tipped with sharp talon-like claws. Like twin shadows they approached the massive, dark hide. Their intended victim could smell the rank odor coming off their bodies and the fetid breath from their open, drooling mouths.

One of the creatures reached out a thick fur-covered arm, snagging the bear skin from the wall as if it was tissue paper. A chorus of barking howls erupted from the pair.

The beautiful Indian woman so coveted by their destroyed shaman, Dream Slayer, stood before them, lush and vulnerable.

These two were in the vanguard that discovered and helped consume the body of the preacher many months before. The taste of the girl was imbedded into their primitive libidos, stirring them both to a near frenzy to mate with her.

Tricia saw their animal lust contort their already ghastly faces, making their hot desire for her flesh burn in the eyes that stroked her body like fevered hands. In their overwhelming drive to have the girl, they failed to see the knives. They gave off a dull glow like burnished gold, yet felt icy in Tricia's hands.

Tricia watched the creatures closely as they inched closer. They panted and grunted in anticipation of their feast. Her back was already to the wall, but the smooth feel of the bone handles in her grip brought an odd sense of calm to her. She raised her head high, meeting their feral eyes. Her jaw set in a determined resolve when she glanced over to see the bear skin stir on the floor beside her.

I will survive, she thought, as she sprang forward.

An enormous roar suddenly filled the lodge in a tidal wave of sound.

The two hunters fell back from the unexpected attack of the flashing knives, only to find themselves facing gaping jaws and twelve feet of angry grizzly.

The bear swept out its front leg like a scythe, nearly sheering the head off a Hunter who had turned to flee. Tricia's knives were deeply imbedded in the heart and throat of the second Hunter. They now glowed a deep crimson as the Hunter twitched with his last breath of life.

She stood looking down at the carnage for a minute before she became aware of the presence standing slightly behind her.

"You have done well, daughter." Shadow Stalker stood where the great bear had only a second earlier. He smiled at Tricia when she looked from him to the inert dark mass of fur lying nearby.

Tricia understood this was the spirit of the great shaman standing before her. He was bathed in the same shimmering glow as the knives, radiating a chill into the air around them.

"Shadow Stalker, you have done me a great honor traveling back from the spirit world in my desperate time of need."

"You are stronger than you perceive, Little Bird. Together, with my grandson, Stone Wolf, you shall serve The People as a Keeper. This is my wish and now your destiny."

Tricia's mind was racing. Questions of how this could be began to spill from her mouth in a torrent of doubt and trepidation.

The shade of the shaman began to falter in its clarity as he held up his nearly transparent hand. "Quiet your heart, Little Bird. This is not a journey you take alone. Your bond with my grandson is strong and will fill you with courage and determination. The People are in need of the Keepers now, more than ever, and you, daughter, shall become the first of your sex to wear the marks of the warrior."

Suddenly, there was a sharp stinging sensation on the backs of her hands. The symbols of the wolf in profile and the burning arrow appeared on the back of each hand.

"I leave you now, Little Bird. Your true heart's mate is nearing. But there is one more thing I must do. These Hunter's will not be gathered by their Spirit Taker while they lie within these sacred walls."

Tricia felt a strong wind rush into the long building. It scoured the floor, sweeping the bodies before it. They fell outside near the stump and within a heartbeat, were claimed by their clan's Spirit Taker.

"Grandfather, will you be with us if we call?"

"Always."

He faded before she could ask anything more.

When she was finally able to control her racing heart, she realized the knives were hanging once again from their pegs on the wall. Their blades were cleansed of blood.

She went outside and sat again on the tree stump. Holding up her hands she studied the new tattoos. It felt right that they were there, marking her status as a Keeper. What would Jack think about this epic change in her life, in their life?

There was no time to worry about his reaction now. The sound of movement through the woods was carried to her ears. Were they more sensitive now, or was she only imagining subtle changes in her senses?

I am a Keeper of The People and will serve with honor, grandfather. In recognition of her promise, she turned to see the great bear shambling through the open doorway. Its massive head turned toward her, beady black eyes holding her in their gaze.

With a subtle shake of its huge head, it wondered off into the dense woods and disappeared among the green shadows.

Chapter 56

Jackson looked over at the couple.

"The lodge is just ahead," he said, encouraging them to move faster.

They followed with more energy now, knowing they would soon be reunited with their daughter.

The outline of the low building was pressed against the thinning trees when Jackson sensed, rather than saw, his love. Forgetting his charges for a moment, he burst through the last shaggy pines. Tricia was standing near the front of the lodge, but ran into his arms the moment she saw him.

He scooped her into his arms and breathed her name close to her ear. With a finger under her chin he lifted her face to his and kissed her deeply. They would have been lost in their embrace, but heard someone clearing their throat to awkwardly announce their presence.

"Mom…Dad!" Tricia tore herself away from a smiling Jackson and ran into the outstretched arms of her parents.

That's when Jackson noticed her hands. He didn't want to say anything with her parents there, but was beside himself with questions. He knew the significance of the tattoos, but couldn't wrap his head around the fact that Tricia was wearing them. How?

Jackson took the opportunity of the other's distraction to enter the lodge, seeking any sign of his grandfather. He knew only the shaman was capable of bestowing those fresh symbols of a Keeper on Tricia.

With the low hum of voices in the background, he stood in the doorway for a moment, letting his eyes adjust. He scanned the long room, accounting for every artifact of their sacred rituals, save one, Shadow Stalker's massive bear hide.

The wall it hung from was empty. His keen eyes made out a faint outline of where the impressive kill had been displayed longer than he could know.

"So, this is your hand I feel, grandfather," he whispered into the shadows.

Not wanting her parents to feel uncomfortable entering the dark building, Jackson quickly lit all the stubby candles he'd left with Tricia. The glow softened the sharp shadows and created a more welcoming atmosphere. He pulled rugs down from various places and arranged them for sitting.

Jackson went outside, moving toward the little circle. They were chatting and smiling with the occasional laugh of sheer happiness.

"Let's go inside so you can visit more comfortably, folks."

Tricia's parents told them how the Tribal Police had no suspects in the killing of the preacher, but were calling it a savage attack by a large predator, likely a puma. If they noticed their daughter's relief at this news, they said nothing.

Her mother was looking at Tricia's hands. She tried to keep them hidden in her lap, but knew she had to satisfy their curiosity.

"My tattoos are a symbol of our commitment to each other," she said reaching for Jackson's hand. This was met with much nodding of their heads in understanding.

The hours slipped by as they talked of their future.

Jackson was watching the shadows lengthen outside the open door. "We need to leave here folks. The sun will set in less than an hour and we have to hike back to the cars before it gets dark."

They made the trek back in less time, being more familiar now with the terrain. After promises of future visits and many tears, the older couple turned their car toward the Res. Tricia watched until the red tail lights were obscured by the distance and trees.

Jackson drove in silence, his arm wrapped around Tricia. He took occasional side glances at her face, now illuminated by the yellow dashboard lights.

She turned toward him, smiling. "I can tell you about what happened at the lodge, Jack."

Tricia finished her story as they pulled into a motel near the airport. They had a 6 a.m. flight back to Chicago's Mid-Way and had already booked a room.

Neither of them moved except for Jackson tightening his grip on Tricia's shoulder.

"Shadow Stalker has chosen you, just as I have, Little Bird. This is not an easy path to follow, but I will be at your side, always."

"That's what Shadow Stalker said to me. Always."

They sat quietly for a moment, wrapped in their own fears and hopes for their future together.

"I know this means we have to return to the Res, Jack. We need to begin my training as a Keeper. Your grandfather told me you would be my teacher."

She gave his hand a light kiss where it cupped her shoulder.

"I won't be afraid anymore. I can feel Shadow Stalker's spirit move through me even now."

He studied her lovely face in the cold blue light from the motel sign. She looked radiant with youth and vitality. But there was something else, something shining from her eyes. He bent his head down to her and they kissed with a new craving and hunger that exceeded anything either had felt before.

In the clarity of that desire, he felt the wolf within her stir.

About the Author

Francesca is part of a large Italian family where she discovered early on that a love of reading was as much a part of her DNA as her mother's skill at baking.

Francesca has worked in local television, a small city zoo, founded a non-profit tutoring agency for an inner-city neighborhood which eventually served local school districts, worked for an International Evangelical Television and Radio Station and for a non-profit organization serving challenged adults.

Francesca Quarto resides in a small town outside of Indianapolis, Indiana with her husband Patrick. She has a great love of the written word and while she enjoys her E-Reader immensely, she still treasures the excitement of turning the next page.

***

Published by Tell-Tale Publishing

www.tell-talepublishing.com